For Dean and Laura

AN ITALIAN COUNT FOR CHRISTMAS

SASHA COTTMAN

Chapter One

C ount Nico de Luca leaned over the side of the ship, the letter crumpled in his hand. Fat raindrops soaked his knuckles. It had rained continually from the moment his ship had sailed into the English Channel.

"Nothing changes in this miserable country," he muttered.

Lifting his head, his gaze took in the dirty, crowded docks of London. He snorted at the sight. As a boy arriving from Italy all those years ago, his first bitter memories of the great English city had been of grey skies and the foul-smelling River Thames.

The stench filled his nostrils and assaulted his mind.

All about him on the deck, the ship's crew were making ready for the ship to berth. The first mate bellowed out a long series of orders. Nico looked up at the captain standing at the ship's helm. The captain gave him a nod of respect in return.

As owner of the ship, it would be easy enough for Nico to simply tell the captain to turn the ship around and sail straight back to Italy. After getting his first glimpse of London in seventeen years, he was sorely tempted to do just that. But a promise was a promise. And Nico de Luca did not make promises lightly.

He looked down at the letter in his hand. It was a brief note. There was little need for Alessandra to say much more than was necessary. She didn't love him, she never had. Her wishes for him to find love and happiness were genuine, Alessandra was not unkind.

"Cheer up Nico. She is not the first woman to have broken your heart. At least she had the decency to break off the betrothal. Be happy for her that she married for love, not just money. Your world has not ended, it just feels like it," he consoled himself.

While he was blessed with the kind of body that would make the angels weep, Nico had been inexplicably cursed in the game of love. At age thirty- two he knew he should be long married and with a home full of children, yet here he was still sailing the seas with no one to share his cabin.

He screwed the letter up into a tight ball, then taking a step backward he pitched it over the side of the ship. There was no use in reading Alessandra's note yet again.

He walked away from the ship's railing but found himself returning to look over the side. He caught sight of the paper as it bobbed on the water one last time before finally disappearing under a dirty brown wave caused by the ship's wake.

He closed his eyes for a moment, feeling at one with the paper that was now on its way to the bottom of the river.

Alessandra was gone, along with her letter. All that remained of their ill- fated love affair were the scars on his heart.

He pushed away from the ship's railing for a second time but this time managed to keep walking. Opening the door of his cabin, the words his father had spoken to him on the dockside in Italy slipped into his mind.

London is where I found your mother, perhaps the love of your life is also waiting for you in England. Do not give up hope Nico. The mother of my grandchildren is somewhere out there, you just need to go and find her.

Frustrated, he pushed the thought away.

"No Papa, I am done with love. Money shall be my mistress from now on. She is steadfast and not fickle like women."

When the time came that he felt he could no longer delay the issue of marriage he would find a kind Italian noble woman to bear his children. He would keep her in jewels and fine clothes and be content. Contentment would have to do. Love he was certain had forsaken him.

Chapter Two

"Ooh."

Isabelle Collins struggled to her feet. Her back ached as did her knees. She looked down at her fingernails. They were chipped and full of dirt.

Nothing of her old life remained. The mark on her left hand from her wedding band had faded away. The ring itself had been sold to pay for firewood.

The only compensation for her aching body and ruined hands was that the dirty marks on the Italian statutory marble fireplace were finally gone. It had taken the best part of a back breaking hour to scrub the marble clean.

The door to the sitting room opened. There was silence for a moment, followed by a loud tsk of disgust. Isabelle didn't bother to turn and face her mother in law, she knew only too well the look which Ann would have on her face.

The same one whenever she mentioned Anthony.

"If that no-good scoundrel of a son of mine wasn't already dead, I would kill him myself," Ann huffed, marching into the room.

Isabelle ignored the remark. She had long ago put away her

dreams of a happy life. Anthony was gone, but the upkeep of the house remained. Unable to afford the luxury of servants it fell to Isabelle and Ann to keep the house clean.

"I have completed everything that I had on my list for today. How about you?" Isabelle replied.

Ann nodded. "Count de Luca's bed is made and his room has been thoroughly dusted. Tomorrow morning, I shall visit the market and get some fresh flowers to put in the vase on his dressing table. Hopefully that should meet with his approval. And if it doesn't there is not a lot I can do about it, we have already spent more than this month's household budget on preparing for our guest's visit. Now put away your cleaning cloths and come and have a well-earned cup of coffee with me," she said.

A loud knock at the front door interrupted their discussion. Isabelle peeked out through the window. A young lad dressed in blue livery stood outside.

"It is a messenger boy," she said.

"I will go. He will want a coin for his trouble and I have some farthings in my pocket," replied Ann.

She returned a minute or so later with a note in her hands, a pensive look on her face.

"It is from his man of business, Mr. Prescott. Apparently, Count de Luca's ship has arrived early into port. He will be joining us later today, not tomorrow. Mr. Prescott sends his apologies, but says he expects we shall manage."

Isabelle pursed her lips. The temporary household staff which Prescott had arranged were not due to arrive until the morning. In the mean time she and Ann would somehow have to cater to the needs of their guest.

"So much for him arriving to a fully maintained and orderly house. At least the cleaning is done. Imagine if he had arrived on our doorstep and I was still scrubbing the fireplaces," replied Isabelle.

Ann cleared her throat as she met Isabelle's gaze.

"Now I know you do not hold with telling falsehoods, but in this case a small white lie might be in order. I do not see any problem with telling our guest that our servants have been delayed on route from our country estate," she said.

Isabelle pondered the hastily cobbled together story and nodded her agreement. Beggars could not be choosers and in this case she and Ann were as close to beggars as anyone she knew. Count De Luca's stay was the long prayed for boon they needed in order to change their reduced circumstances. After having lived for two years on the knife's edge of financial ruin Isabelle was no longer tightly wedded to her moral code. If lying was what it took in order to reclaim her old life Isabelle Collins was prepared to tell a great many lies.

"Yes. On a whim we decided to come to town a day or two early. What a silly pair we are in having forgotten that the house would not be ready for our arrival. Our servants were left at home," said Isabelle with a smile.

Servants. The very word held the promise of a change in their lives. One thing she was certain of was that when she finally did get back onto the marriage market she would be setting her sights squarely on potential husbands who had the means to maintain a whole house of paid staff.

"It will be so nice to have a house full of servants again, even if only for a few weeks. My back could certainly do with a rest from cleaning. Oh, to be a lady of leisure once more," said Ann.

Isabelle wiped her hands on her apron. Her father would turn in his grave if he could see the life his beloved daughter was now living. He had given her the choice of marrying for love, and in Anthony Collins she had thought to have found the perfect husband. The bitter years which followed had taught her otherwise.

She forced the regret away. A small allowance from Ann's own marriage settlement covered the rent on the house. Isabelle contributed a few pounds a year from the grace of a distant relative. They had one poorly paid cook who steadfastly refused to leave their employ. The household barely made ends meet, neither woman ever giving voice to the fear of what would happen to them when one of life's disasters eventually befell them.

Ann folded up the note and tucked it into the pocket of her apron.

"Well, let us go and have a moment of peace before our guest arrives. With any luck he will be tired from his long sea voyage and wish to retire to his room to sleep. By the time he wakes the servants will have arrived."

Isabelle followed Ann toward the door.

"Just remember thirty days. No matter what he demands of us, he will be gone in thirty days," she said.

Ann looked back over her shoulder.

"Thirty-one. He is a day early."

Chapter Three

Nico climbed down from the coach outside number seventy-four New Cavendish Street and stood taking in the view.

The house was a simple white building, constructed over four floors from the street, with a lower ground floor for the kitchens and servants' area. The plain black front door spoke of a well ordered and maintained dwelling. Two purple magnolia bushes grew either side of the front door, their higher branches elegantly trailed up the walls and past the first two rows of windows. They crossed over at the top of each row of windows forming a pleasant cross stitch pattern.

He nodded his approval. He liked his investments to be well looked after; it helped to keep their value. The house and its well-kept appearance did little however to lift his black mood.

His early arrival into port meant there was no carriage waiting for him when the ship docked. The ship's captain had sent word immediately to the offices of the de Luca shipping company, but it had been over an hour before he and his luggage had been loaded up into a hastily arranged coach and taken to New Cavendish Street.

After a few minutes of standing out in the street he began to impatiently tap his gloved hand against the side of his coat. Word of his early arrival must surely have been sent ahead by now and the tenants be all in readiness for his arrival.

He glared at the front door, silently commanding it to open. When the door did not open and the expected butler appear he made a mental note to have a firm word with the man about his tardiness. Guests should not have to wait out in the street when they were expected. He was a member of one of Italy's greatest noble families, and he did not wait for anyone.

In frustration he finally marched up to the front door and rapped loudly on the door knocker. After a few more minutes, which had seen his temper slowly build to boiling point, the door finally opened. A young woman, with an apron over her plain black gown answered the door.

She looked from Nico to the coachman standing behind him and frowned.

"Oh," she said.

"Oh indeed!" he snapped.

He marched into the house, forcing Isabelle to step aside. The gruff driver of the coach followed behind. He muttered various curses under his breath as he carried the heavy luggage into the house. He deposited several large travel bags onto the black and white tiled foyer floor before standing hands on hips and glaring at Isabelle.

Nico could hear the man's breath being sucked furiously in and out of his teeth. The coachman then marched back out into the street.

He turned to Isabelle.

"Signorina, I think you need to go and find the butler or at least a useful footman. Someone has to bring the rest of my luggage inside. I am damned if I am going to do it," he said.

When Ann appeared from out of the ground floor sitting room

he gave a sigh of relief. From her manner of dress and the way she held herself it was clear she was not one of the servants.

Finally.

"Good morning your excellency, welcome to our home," she said.

A relived Nico took off his hat and promptly handed it and his gloves to Isabelle. She accepted them somewhat awkwardly. Nico dipped into a low bow and addressed Ann.

"Count Nico de Luca of the noble house of Lazio. I am pleased to make your acquaintance madam. I was just explaining to your maid here that she had better find some other servants to help bring my travel trunk inside. I have been made to wait outside in the street for some time and my patience has been sorely tested," he said.

Ann cleared her throat, while Isabelle looked down at the floor.

"My lord, I am Ann Collins. I offer you my most sincere apologies for our lack of preparedness for your arrival. We only received word a short while ago that your ship had made port a day early. If you would be so kind as to come into the sitting room for a moment, I shall make the necessary arrangements to have your luggage brought inside."

Nico caught the edge of disapproval in her voice as she pointed to the doorway from where she had just appeared. He was suddenly reminded of his mother and how she had dealt with displays of ill manners. He muttered under his breath at the unexpected rebuke.

Meanwhile the angry coachman reappeared carrying several more bags and a tall thin wooden box.

"I told you to be careful with the box," said Nico, as the luggage was deposited unceremoniously onto the floor.

The coachman gave him a filthy look before turning on his heel and marching back out into the street.

"My lord?"

Nico turned and followed Ann.

☙

Isabelle followed the ill-tempered coachman out the front door of the house and watched as he climbed aboard his coach and departed. His bad manners had at least saved her the coins for the usual tip and for that she was grateful.

He had however left her a parting gift. To one side of the front door stood an enormous travel trunk. It was almost as tall as Isabelle. At the sight of the travel trunk her heart sank. How the devil was she going to get it inside on her own? She turned at the sound of footsteps behind her.

"Sorry about that. He thinks you are a house maid. I gave him an apple and told him I would arrange refreshments, Mrs. Brown is brewing a pot of tea. What is that?" said Ann, pointing to the travel trunk.

"His travel trunk by the look of it. It must weight half a hundred-weight. I have absolutely no idea how we are going to get it inside, I just know we cannot leave it out here in the street. The neighbors will pitch a fit," replied Isabelle.

She looked the trunk up and down praying it would suddenly grow legs and walk into the house of its own accord. It would be impossible to drag it up the front steps and inside without damaging the bottom of the trunk.

"You shall have to take one end and I the other. We will manage as best we can. There is nothing else to be done," said Ann.

Isabelle nodded. For the past two years they had always managed to find a way to make things work, today was no different. She rubbed her already tired knees and tried not to think how much they would ache by tomorrow morning.

Reaching up she placed her hands on the top of the travel trunk and pulled it down toward her. She spread her feet and steadied her grip. Ann stood at the other end of the trunk.

"One. Two. Three and lift."

The travel trunk was as heavy as it looked. Within seconds of picking it up and staggering a few steps they had to set it down again.

"What has he got in there?" Isabelle muttered.

They picked the travel trunk up a second time, made several more steps toward the front door, then set it down again. Isabelle stood in the street hands on hips sucking in air. Ann simply shook her head. Isabelle offered her an encouraging smile while wiping her hands on her apron.

"Come on, only a few more steps and we shall have this monstrous beast across the threshold," she said.

She had just put her hands under the travel trunk, ready to lift it a third time when Nico suddenly appeared at her shoulder.

"What the devil are you doing young woman?" he asked.

"Bringing your trunk inside," she replied flatly.

He waved his hands in the air and the women stepped away from the trunk. He snorted a loud huff of disgust and turned to Ann.

"Where are your man servants and footmen madam? Since when did housemaids and ladies have to carry heavy luggage? This won't do," he said.

Ann came around to where Isabelle stood.

"Our servants are on route from our country estate, we were not expecting you until tomorrow, my apologies. My lord, we are trying to manage as best we can," she replied.

Isabelle took personal satisfaction on seeing the uncomfortable look which appeared on the Nico's face.

Rude pompous swine.

"I see. Well since there is nothing to be done about your absent servants I suggest that the two of you take the other end of the trunk together. I shall take this end and we will see how we go. Just remember to let me know if you need to set it down if it becomes too heavy a burden," he said.

With the women at one end and Nico at the other the task of

lifting the trunk became much easier. They soon lifted it up the front steps and into the house.

As they went to set the trunk down in the hallway, their shortly lived good fortune failed them. Isabelle's sweaty hands lost their grip and the edge of the trunk landed heavily on Nico's foot.

"Oh! Porca miseria!" he cried, as he danced about the front entrance of the house in pain.

Isabelle didn't understand what he was saying, but she had an inkling it would not translate well into English.

Ann rushed to the front door and closed it behind her. Isabelle caught a snippet of her muttering something about the neighbors and what they would think.

For herself she had given up caring what other people said about the goings on at number seventy- four. And as for bad tempered Count de Luca, she couldn't help but think that he had got exactly what he deserved.

"I am so sorry your excellency. I didn't mean to drop it that quickly," said Isabelle, masking her true feelings.

The morning was quickly turning from bad to worse.

"I can get a cold compress for your foot if you wish," she offered.

Nico waved her offer away.

"No, my foot is fine. Just a little pain, nothing feels broken. Not yet anyway," he snapped.

Ann headed toward the stairs which led down into the lower kitchen.

"Excuse me while I leave the two of you to get acquainted. I must check on the cook and that cup of tea," she said.

As Ann departed Isabelle removed her apron and wiped her hands on it. She caught the odd look on Nico's face and smiled.

"No, my mother in law is not mad, she didn't leave you to socialize with the house maid. I am Isabelle Collins, your tenant. You caught us in the middle of tidying up in preparation for your arrival. You are early, hence the lack of a formal welcome," she said.

She curtseyed elegantly to him reflecting her own well-bred

status. She was surprised to be rewarded with a warm smile when she caught his gaze once more. Deep brown eyes greeted her. Eyes that sparkled when he smiled.

Nico bowed low in return.

"Count Nico de Luca, at your service Mrs. Collins. My sincere apologies for my early arrival and any inconvenience it may cause. My ship made good time coming up the coast of Portugal and we arrived a day or so early in London. It was thoughtless of me to arrive at such short notice and make demands of your household. I am tired but as a gentleman that does not excuse my rude behavior," he replied.

Isabelle looked at him, lost for words. She had not had much to do with society since the death of her husband and couldn't remember the last time a gentleman had visited the house. She suddenly felt sheepish at her own unkind thoughts of the count.

Count de Luca was not how she had imagined him. He was a lot younger for a start, perhaps only a few years older than herself. Handsome was the next word which came to mind. Devilishly handsome.

She studied him for a moment. There was something about his appearance that had her wondering as to his family background. He was taller than other European gentleman she had met in her life. He towered over her, his physical presence dominating the space between them. A space that was heating up by the second.

His jet-black hair and dark brown eyes reminded her of a Titian painting she had once seen while attending a ball at the home of the Earl of Harrington. There was a warmth about him that even his ill temper could not hide.

And that sensual accent. It was Italian, but his English was flawless. When he cleared his throat. Isabelle felt a rush of heat to her cheeks. She had been silently staring at her guest.

"Not quite the continental gentleman you had been expecting?" he asked.

Mortified, she died a little more inside. She could only hope that he hadn't taken offence at her staring at him.

"I went to school here in England for several years; and my mother was English if that helps to clear up any confusion. I am told I look more English than Roman, but my father says I have the heart of a Roman and that is what truly matters," he added.

Isabelle stifled an 'Oh'. She had been about to comment on his excellent command of the English language. At least he had saved her from making that embarrassing faux pas.

"So, you do have a cook? Or is the other Mrs. Collins downstairs trying to light the fire and boil the water herself?" he asked.

Isabelle would have taken offence at his remark had she not seen the grin which appeared on Nico's lips. He was teasing her.

"We have a cook my lord," she replied.

He nodded. "Molto bene. But since this is your home Isabella, please call me Nico. I should like to think that once we have over-come the awkward introductions we will be friends. I must thank you for making the generous offer to host me while I am in London. I was not looking forward to spending Christmas by myself in a hotel. I promise after this false start I shall not be a burden."

Isabelle stood listening to his words, letting the curl of his Italian accent caress her. She had always had a soft spot for men with a foreign accent. She particularly liked the way that Nico called her Isabella, with the soft bella on the end. She had no intention whatso-ever in correcting his pronunciation of her name.

Ann returned, to Isabelle's disappointment. She was enjoying her private moment with their handsome guest.

"Your tea will be ready shortly my lord. If you like I could show you to your room where you could freshen up," offered Ann.

"Thank you Mrs. Collins I would like to find a place for my coat and things," he replied.

After showing Nico to his room, Ann returned a few minutes later and took Isabelle aside. "Well this is going to be an interesting Christmas. He wants us to call him Nico. He is not at all what I was expecting. For a start he couldn't be much older than thirty, and he is rather dashing. I swear from the moment he stepped across the threshold I was ready to fall into his magnificent brown eyes. And he hasn't yet made mention of a wife or family. I'm beginning to wonder if our count is a bachelor."

Isabelle raised an eyebrow at her mother in law. Ann had been alone with Nico for all of five minutes and yet he was already their count. She didn't need to ask why Ann was so interested in Nico's marital status. An unmarried Italian nobleman was the stuff of every widow's dreams.

She shook her head. If she didn't take charge, Ann would be making arrangements for Isabelle to become the Contessa de Luca before the year was out.

"I expect his wife did not want to come all the way to England for Christmas and is staying at home in Rome with their brood of beautiful sable- haired children," she replied.

Ann began to hum softly to herself.

Isabelle stood and stared at her. Ann only hummed like that when she was up to something.

"What?"

A soft smile appeared on Ann's lips and she reached out and patted Isabelle gently on the arm.

"You know I love you as my own daughter. So, when the count mentioned that he was looking for someone who could show him around London to help reacquaint himself with the city. I well...," said Ann.

"You didn't."

"I did. I offered him your services."

Isabelle sighed. Ann was already one step ahead of her.

Chapter Four

Nico wandered around his bedroom for a minute or so after Ann left. He sat on the bed and spread his arms wide. The empty vase which stood on the nearby dresser caught his eye. Why the English were afraid of color was something that he had never understood. He would venture out in the morning and buy some fresh flowers to brighten the room.

His feet touched the floor. It was good to finally be back on dry land. It would take a day or so for his brain to register the fact that he was no longer at sea and for his feet to stop mimicking the rolling motion of the ship.

His cabin on board the ship had been well appointed and by ship's standards spacious. Being the owner of the ship did have its benefits.

A soft tap on the bedroom door roused him from his musings. Clambering off the bed he opened the door.

Isabelle entered carrying a small tray.

"Your tea and a piece of Mrs. Brown's Madeira cake. If there is anything else you would like, please let me know and we shall endeavor to bring it to you," she said.

She set the tray down on the bedside table, then turned to face him with hands clasped in front of her.

"I must apologize for my state of attire when you arrived earlier. It was entirely my fault that you thought I was a maid. And may I also apologize once more for your foot. If you need a doctor, I can summon one for you," she said.

In the light from the nearby window, Nico got his first real look at Isabelle. With the apron gone, he could see her slender waist to advantage. Her breasts though constrained by her gown, still showed themselves to be ample. He was a man with a keen eye for a woman's breasts. The widow Collins was pleasingly well endowed.

A primal reaction to her stirred in his body. His mouth went dry as he watched her studying him.

He delighted in the thought that her gaze was not innocent. Whether she realized it or not, she was slowly stripping him naked with her deep green eyes. His breathing grew shorter as he felt revealed to her.

He swallowed deep as his gaze took in the rose color of her mouth. A mouth that begged a man to nibble and taste of its sweet lips. Lips he was certain were in need of a thorough kissing.

He caught himself before his imagination could indulge in the fantasy of what Isabelle would look like naked and laying beneath him.

"My foot is fine, thank you Isabella. I shall take a short stroll later to check that it is still in one piece."

She blushed. Nico struggled to hold back a sexual response to the heat on her cheeks.

Get a hold of yourself. You have been in this woman's home all of five minutes and you are already having lascivious thoughts of her. What happened to your vow of being done with women. Done with love.

She was his tenant. A respectable widow from what Prescott had told him in his letter. His thoughts of what he would like to do to her were however far from respectable.

A hotel might be a better option.

"My mother in law tells me that I am to accompany you around London as your guide. I trust that meets with your agreement. If not, I could find a gentleman to do the task," she said.

Disappointment stirred in his heart. Isabelle Collins was a far more enticing prospect for showing him the sights of dreary London than a man. A man would want to show him his club or his horses. A woman would be open to art galleries and music. And shopping.

Nico was a lover of many things. Music and dance called to his Italian soul but being in London he itched to work his way through the array of shops on Oxford Street. Women were always a delight to take shopping. Alessandra had been appreciative of his talents when it came to buying her lavish gifts. Talents she rewarded with allowing Nico to unwrap her gown once he accompanied her home at end of their shopping trips.

His mind was already wondering how many shopping trips it would take before he could entice the widow Collins to unwrap herself for him.

"No, I am happy for you to show me the sights. Mrs. Collins tells me you are a native of London and know all the right places to visit. It has been many years since I lived in England, so having a local guide will be invaluable. I promise not to take up too much of your time," he replied.

He had not been all that too concerned when Ann Collins first offered for Isabelle to accompany him around London, a guide was a means to an end. But having now seen her up close and gained an appreciation of her fresh beauty, Nico wanted to have her by his side.

"Well then we have an accord. When do you wish for us to undertake our first outing?" she asked.

"Tomorrow?" he ventured. The sooner he got more acquainted with her the better.

"Tomorrow it is, please enjoy your tea before it gets cold. If you need anything for the rest of today, you may wish to come downstairs. Unfortunately, your travel trunk will have to reside downstairs until tomorrow when the rest of the servants arrive," said Isabelle.

She left Nico alone with his rapidly cooling tea and spongy cake. He crossed the floor to where the bag with his personal papers was sitting. The tall wooden box had been placed safely against the wall.

"I need light," he muttered.

Spotting a small table in the corner, he carried it over to the window where he set it down. Retrieving his satchel of papers, he emptied its contents onto the table.

Within a short time, he had his papers in ordered piles on the desk. His paper and ink were set out just the way he liked them. After placing a chair under the table, he stood back and surveyed his work.

"Molto bene," he said.

Everything was ready and in its place. He could sit at his desk and observe the English rain while working on his business letters. Sightseeing in London had been a secondary priority before his arrival but having now met his tempting travel guide he felt a sudden urgency to play tourist.

"So much for giving up on women," he chuckled.

His resolve to harden his heart against the prospect of love had lasted less than a day.

Chapter Five

"What a lovely gown my dear Isabelle. Is it new?"

Isabelle stopped mid frown when she saw Nico rise from his chair in the downstairs sitting room the following morning. He gave her an elegant bow, which had heat racing to her cheeks.

"You look stunning," he said.

If he had not been present she would have reminded Ann that the gown was at least three seasons old, which she well knew.

The happy smile on Ann's face explained the reason for her comment. Isabelle was not dressed in black and she was about to spend a day out on the town with a gentleman. A rich handsome Italian gentleman.

"Thank you. I wasn't sure about the gown, but the dressmaker convinced me to buy it," she replied, adding another white lie to the growing list.

Isabelle was dressed in a pale purple gown with grey and white stripes down the skirt. Anthony had bought it for her during one of his rare runs of luck with the cards. She didn't particularly like it, but the gown was warm.

It was early December and the weather had already turned to

winter. On her daily walk to the market Isabelle had seen people venturing out onto the frozen sections of the River Thames to ice skate.

"Are you sure you won't join us today Mrs. Collins? The carriage I have hired has plenty of room, you would be most welcome," said Nico.

Ann shook her head.

"The staff began arriving early this morning and I want to be home to ensure that they get settled back into their routines as soon as possible. Our butler will act as your valet during your stay," she replied.

The glint in Ann's eyes at the thought of having a household of servants again brought joy to Isabelle's heart. She knew that within minutes of her and Nico's departure that Ann would be marshalling the household staff and making sure they understood their duties. She couldn't begrudge Ann her amusement. The day after Nico departed, the servants would be gone and the Collins women would go back to their quiet life of cleaning and dusting.

The weight of expectation of her securing a new favorable marriage in the coming year sat heavily on her shoulders.

She looked once more at Nico, and Isabelle's eyes lit up.

He was like something out of a renaissance painting. His pale brown skin no longer held the tired look of one who had been on a long journey. His eyes sparkled in the morning light, reflecting warmth and charm.

"I trust you slept well last night my lord," she asked.

Oh, my you are lovely. How your wife could have ever let you travel alone to England is beyond me.

"I did thank you. The bed was a great relief from the constant rolling of the ship. But please call me Nico," he replied.

Ann rose from her seat and took hold of Isabelle's arm.

"I was just telling Nico about all the places you wanted to show him. Floris perfumery was first on your list of shops was it not my dear?"

Isabelle kept her gaze firmly on Nico, but silently nodded. She had actually planned a trip to Hyde Park and around Buckingham Palace, but she was too lost in staring at the magnificent man who stood before her to bother correcting Ann.

"Ah so you think I need to update my cologne, do you?" asked Nico.

Isabelle shook herself awake from her pleasant day dream.

"Yes. I mean no. I."

He chuckled at her obvious embarrassment. The deep tone of his laughter filled her heart with unexpected joy. She couldn't recall the last time anyone had genuinely laughed in the house.

"Never mind. I am just happy to be off the boat and able to walk around without getting a face full of salt water spray. If you wish our first visit to be to a perfumery, then so be it. Shall we go?"

Isabelle looked at Nico's offered arm and a nervous bubble popped in her stomach. How she had missed the simple pleasure of being out in society with a gentleman.

Ann ushered them both quickly out the sitting room and handed Isabelle her cloak. Isabelle stifled a laugh as Ann beat the newly arrived butler to the task of opening the front door. Isabelle and Nico were outside on the front steps in quick time.

As they stepped out into the street, Isabelle's eyes grew wide. Standing waiting for them was an elegant carriage, the likes of which she had only ever seen carrying members of the royal family. It was black and had two colorful flags flying from the front of the roof just behind the driver.

The driver himself and the rest of the team were all decked out in matching livery of gold and red. A pair of servants stood at the back of the carriage, both wearing tall hats decorated with gold and red feathers.

Isabelle turned to Nico, who smiled at her.

"The Lazio family crest is emblazoned on the pennants. Red and gold are the traditional color of Rome and his Holiness the Pope," explained Nico.

Isabelle imagined herself a fairy princess about to ride off in her carriage. Forgetting her manners entirely she hastened her step, eager to climb inside. Before she got to the carriage however Nico pulled her back.

"Now my mother, had three rules for leaving the house. And since this is my carriage we shall continue to follow them. The first one, never been in too much of a hurry to take your leave of your home. Walk elegantly toward your carriage in order to permit the neighbors a better look of both your posture and attire. New clothes should be gifted with a sense of occasion on their first public outing," he said.

Isabelle looked at him for a moment, unsure as to whether he was in jest or not. He nodded sagely toward her.

"Secondly, travel in the finest carriage money can buy. Forget bloodlines, people always judge you by your coach or carriage."

He took her hand and helped her up into the carriage. She waved to Ann who remained standing on the front steps, a look of triumph on her face.

As the footman closed the door behind them, Isabelle took her seat. Nico took the seat opposite. Isabelle fixed her cloak and skirts before finally meeting his gaze.

"And the third rule?" she asked.

He put his hand inside his coat and pulled out a small silver hipflask. He handed it to her.

"Always carry good brandy on your person, you never know when you might need a nip or two."

A wicked smile crept to his lips. Isabelle sat and stared at him for a moment, before lifting the hip flask to her lips.

"That is good brandy, it warms you to the toes. Thank you. Tell me does your mother really have those rules?" she said handing him back the hip flask.

He smiled as he slipped the hip flask back into his coat pocket.

"The first two were set in stone, the last one I added myself. My mother loved to make a grand statement whenever she left the house. Even her funeral was considered a showy affair by Roman standards," he replied.

The smile disappeared from his face and Isabelle sensed a change in his mood. "I'm sorry for your loss. How long ago did your mother die?" she asked.

Her own recent experience with bereavement had taught her that talking about the deceased made it easier to cope.

"We lost her earlier this year, some six months ago," he replied.

Isabelle reached out and placed a hand on his arm.

"I had no idea. It must be very difficult to be away from home at this time of the year. Christmas is always a time for family. If there is anything I can do to make your stay more comfortable you only have to ask."

Nico touched his fingers to her hand before she moved it away.

"Thank you. I know we made plans to visit the scent makers this morning, but would it be acceptable for us to visit Fortnum and Mason's first thing instead? I have a strong craving for scotch eggs and they do make the very best of them. We could go on to Floris' afterwards," he replied.

Isabelle sat back and looked at him. He was an odd mixture of Italian and English gentleman. There was a passion about him that could only come from being European, while at the same time he had an endearing habit of saying things that could only come from being an Englishman.

She had skipped breakfast in order to spend longer this morning on setting her hair. Instead of the usual practical bun, her chestnut hair had been set in a soft chignon with trailing curls which kissed her cheeks.

The offer of freshly made scotch eggs was all too tempting.

"Agreed but only if you tell my mother in law that Floris's were not open when we arrived. I would hate to disappoint her by changing her plans," she replied.

The carriage made its way down to Piccadilly and stopped out the front of the tall red brick shop of Fortnum and Mason. Isabelle put her face up against the glass as they drew to a halt.

Nico stepped down from the carriage and had his attendants stand to attention as he assisted Isabelle down the carriage steps. She found herself smiling at several people who stopped and took in the sight of the magnificent carriage.

Nico leaned in close and whispered. "Now, pretend to ignore them as you walk inside. The secret of a great entrance is not to be self-conscious."

Isabelle sucked in a deep breath and prayed she didn't trip over her feet on the way into the shop.

Once inside Nico revealed himself to be no stranger to Fortnum and Mason. Taking Isabelle by the arm, he made a beeline for the food hall counter where they sold all manner of picnic hamper delights.

His gaze ran eagerly over the contents of the glass display case and the various baskets of freshly baked goods which sat on top of the counter.

"Ah potted crab, my heart's delight!" he exclaimed, picking up a jar.

Isabelle failed to stifle a laugh. Nico was like a small excited boy in the body of an Adonis. His enthusiasm was infectious.

"Two of those please, and don't bother wrapping them," he said, pointing at a tray of scotch eggs.

As soon as the shop assistant placed the eggs on the counter Nico snatched them up. Grinning with delight he handed one to Isabelle before taking a large bite of his own egg.

The assistant and Isabelle exchanged a bemused look before she followed Nico's lead and took a bite of her egg. The cold cooked sausage and boiled egg were a heavenly combination.

As Nico took the last bite of his egg, he held up a finger pointing to the rest of the eggs.

"All of them sir?" asked the shop assistant.

Nico swallowed down the rest of his egg.

"Yes, and a selection of the rest of the hamper goods if you would be so kind. Put them all in one of your special baskets. My footman will take it to our carriage," he replied.

❧

Nico made a show of examining the rest of the food hall counters, but all the while he was watching Isabelle out of the corner of his eye. She appeared overwhelmed by the shop. Her gaze darting constantly back and forth.

"Do you have any favorite places within the shop?" he asked.

Isabelle shook her head but her gaze remained fixed on a nearby cabinet of sweet treats. Nico caught the eye of the shop assistant and pointed to the cakes.

"Three of all of those as well thank you," he said.

He found himself suddenly taken aback at Isabelle's response to his generosity. Her demeanor turned to one of guarded wariness. He knew the signals only too well.

He privately chided himself for being too ostentatious. His cack-handed attempt to befriend Isabelle had been taken by her as an uncivilized display of wealth and privilege. The English frowned upon such crass behavior.

He leaned in close and looked into her eyes.

"Have I over stepped the boundaries of good taste? My mother always said that I have a habit of getting a little carried away at times," he said.

Her countenance immediately softened at his self-reproach, and he took heart.

"No of course not. It is wonderful to see someone who loves their fine food as much as you obviously do. I am just not accustomed to such exuberant behavior," she replied.

He stopped himself from taking hold of her hand. She was skittish enough without imposing himself further on her. They stood for a moment in silence while the shop assistants went about the business of wrapping and packing Nico's purchases.

"I don't suppose they deliver hampers as far as your home in the country. Where did you say your estate was?" he asked, attempting a different tack.

He caught the sudden stiffening of her posture at his question. When she swallowed deep, he silently cursed himself for having once more crossed her personal boundary.

Nico was not used to this response from a woman. In Rome women fought one another to gain his favor. Flirting with Count Nico de Luca was considered a sport among the married women of the noble houses of the papacy. To be invited to join him on one of his shopping expeditions was considered a major triumph. That and what followed after.

"Wiltshire," she finally replied.

Isabelle moved away from him. She stopped at a counter selling honey and engaged in an intense conversation with the attendant about the provenance of the various honeys. Nico decided it was best to leave her alone for a moment. When Isabelle finally re-joined him, she was carrying a small parcel in her hands.

"Ann so does love the honey from Fortnum's, she has it on her bread for breakfast every day," she said.

Nico noted the distinct cooling in the friendly relationship that had existed earlier in the morning. Isabelle was hiding something from him, he just wasn't sure what.

Or for that matter why.

"Could I treat you to some tea and cake? You must be acquainted with some of the nearby places, or we could go to Gunter's in Berkeley Square that was one of my favorites when I lived in England," he offered.

Tears appeared in Isabelle's eyes and she hurriedly looked down at the small parcel in her hands.

"I think perhaps I should like to get this jar of honey home to Ann. I am a tad clumsy at times, and I would hate for something to happen to it. We could pay a visit to Gunter's at another time," she replied.

Being in possession of three sisters, Nico knew not to push his luck when it came to young women and their sudden changes in mood. Isabelle was clearly uncomfortable and wanted to go home. As a gentleman, and more importantly a guest in her house he had a responsibility to abide by her wishes.

"As you wish. The carriage is at our disposal for the duration of my stay, so we shall have plenty of opportunities to sample the delights of London," he replied.

Chapter Six

After arriving home from their shortened day trip Nico was greeted with one piece of good news. The rest of the servants had now arrived and his travel trunk was no longer taking up space downstairs.

Isabelle bade him a hurried farewell and headed upstairs.

"I am sorry for cutting short our trip today. I feel a headache coming on and I wouldn't be very good company if we remained in the city. I shall give this jar of honey to Ann then retire to my room," she said.

With the arrival of the servants there was now a hum about the house that had been lacking upon his arrival. The footman from his coach handed the hamper basket from Fortnum and Mason to the butler, who in turn handed it to another footman. A maid took it downstairs to the kitchen. Nico raised an eyebrow at the obvious pecking order which was in place.

The butler dipped into a low bow.

"My lord. Mrs. Collins has asked that I double as your valet for the duration of your stay. As such I have unpacked your travel trunk and hung your clothes in the wardrobe. I have also pressed your dinner jackets and shirts," he said.

"Excellent. You have been busy since your arrival. I would have thought you would be weary from the long journey," replied Nico.

The butler scowled.

"Surrey is only a few miles away my lord, we left the estate early this morning," he replied.

Nico held back on commenting on the man's response. Isabelle had mentioned Wiltshire as where the family estate was situated, yet the butler had said Surrey.

He wasn't by nature a suspicious man, but the butler's response coupled with Isabelle's sudden need to return home had him wondering.

"Very good. I shall be visiting my man of business later today, but I don't have any plans as yet for the evening. I shall inform you if that situation changes," he replied.

Nico headed upstairs intending to go to his room. On the first floor, he saw the door to the formal drawing room was open. Voices drifted out into the hallway from within.

"What are we to do? If he takes me to more shops I will be obliged to buy goods which we can barely afford. I am beginning to think we didn't put enough thought into having the count stay with us," said Isabelle.

Nico stopped in the hallway and looked around. There were no servants to be seen. With soft, slow steps he crept closer to the door of the drawing room.

"Nonsense, we will have funds soon enough. You can buy a few things here and there, just don't spend too much money. The servants are here now, so he would have no reason to think we have little money to our name," replied Ann.

Nico leaned against the wall and continued to listen.

"Yes, well he asked about our country estate today, and he caught me off guard," replied Isabelle.

"What did you say?"

"My mind went blank and I said Wiltshire. I know we had agreed on Surrey, but I panicked," said Isabelle.

At the sound of approaching footsteps on the staircase Nico hurried away from the doorway and to his room. Once inside he closed the door behind him and considered the events of the morning.

The situation made no sense. If the Collins women were indeed poor as church mice then why had they agreed to let him stay with them over Christmas? And where were they getting the money to maintain a household of servants?

He ran his thumb over the silver eagle set in gold which adorned the top of his signet ring and pondered the puzzle of the Collins' home. When he finally stepped away from the door, he was sure of only one thing. Nico would bet a box of silver papal scudos that if asked, the servants would have little idea beyond a name as to who Ann and Isabelle Collins were.

"Well that is a mystery," he muttered.

With his travel trunk now in his room he opened the last of the locked drawers and took out several large folders of paper. He rang the bell for the butler.

"Would you please arrange for the carriage to be brought around from the stables at five o'clock. I will be visiting my man of business at Wapping Dock. I am not certain what time I shall return, so please let either of the two Mrs. Collins know that I shall not require supper."

The morning's outing with Isabelle had been a pleasant distraction, but he had business to attend to while in London. The intriguing matter of the financial situation of the tenants of seventy-four New Cavendish Street would have to wait.

Chapter Seven

Isabelle stayed in her room until she heard Nico leave for his late afternoon appointment. Having a stranger in the house was more confronting that she had expected it to be. One of the new footmen greeted her at the bottom of the stairs.

"His lordship left you this madam," he said, handing her a note.

She took it, surprised at how uncertain she felt at receiving it. Her fingers trembled as she unfolded the paper. She looked up to see Ann coming up from the kitchen.

> *Dear Mrs. Collins,*
> *I offer my sincerest apologies for being so forward this*
> *morning during our outing. My behavior made you*
> *uncomfortable and for that I am deeply sorry.*
> *It would appear that I am a source of discomfort to you. I*
> *shall not intrude upon your time in future and shall*
> *maintain a more gentleman like decorum when in your*
> *presence.*
> *I have a business meeting to attend to early this evening and*
> *will likely dine out before I return. I shall make every*

*endeavor not to make any disturbance when I return to
the house.*

*If you do however find that I am imposing upon your good
self, I shall remove myself to a hotel at the earliest
convenience.*

Your humble servant

Nico de Luca

"What does it say?" asked Ann.

She pulled the paper out of Isabelle's grasp. A loud *tsk* of disapproval came from her lips as she read the note.

"This will not do! We cannot have him feeling that he is imposing on us. The last thing we need is for him to up stumps and go to a hotel. Prescott will have the servants out of the house in a flash, and our plans to use the extra money to launch you back into society will come to naught. Isabelle you need to encourage his friendship. Or at the very least don't make him feel unwelcome," she said.

Isabelle pursed her lips. Ann was right. Without the money they would save in rent, they would never be able to have the means to see her settled into a new marriage. She had behaved like a green school room miss today and jeopardized their plans.

"What am I to do?" she replied.

"You will be nice to him and show him London as we agreed. He shouldn't be the one apologizing. Did you see all the delightful treats he bought us in that hamper? Tomorrow morning you shall go and speak to him. Tell him you were feeling a little unwell today, and that you are eager to be his city guide. And if he wishes to be generous to you with his money, then for heaven's sake let him," said Ann.

Chapter Eight

N ico stepped out of the carriage clutching his satchel under his arm. It was stuffed full of papers. Making notes on his various investments on the sea voyage from Italy had kept the thought of Alessandra from his mind for some of the time.

The dock area where the de Luca shipping offices were situated was a hive of activity. Wagons laden with barrels and crates of goods rolled past as he stood on the side of Wapping Street and took in the view. The recently completed Wapping Dock was exactly how he had hoped it would look.

Ships were able to dock and unload their goods with greater efficiency than before. Days spent in port cost ship owners like him valuable time and money. With the war in Europe now over and its new offices situated close to the docks, the de Luca shipping company was set to expand its trade operations.

He walked up to the front door of number thirty- seven Wapping Street and was greeted by the doorman. The doorman was a short man dressed in a dark green uniform with matching top hat. He possessed the requisite stern look which would ensure that only those with valid business ties with the de Luca shipping company would succeed in crossing the threshold. Upon seeing Nico, he cleared his throat and dropped into a low bow.

"Your Serene Excellency," said the man.

Nico stifled a grin. He would have to remember to tell his father about the new title his son had been gifted while in England.

The thought of his father pulled him out of the moment. Lorenzo would soon be facing his first Christmas without his beloved Elizabeth. Had his eldest son made a mistake in leaving Rome at such a time?

His musings were cut short by the arrival of a well- dressed man who descended down a nearby staircase.

"Ah, your lordship. Welcome. We have been expecting you."

Nico noted the odd absence of a bow from his business manager. He barely nodded his head in acknowledgement of Nico's status.

"Phillip Prescott at your service. After all these years it is good to finally meet you."

Prescott turned to the doorman. "Would you please organize fresh coffee for the count and myself. We shall be in my office. Thank you, Mr. Fisher."

Nico followed his business manager back up the stairs and into the office. As soon as he stepped into the room, he was struck by its lavish decorations and expensive furnishings. The walls were lined with mahogany paneling and on one hung a Chinese silk tapestry.

The desk on which Nico set his papers was bigger than the one he had in Rome. The ornate carvings on its legs spoke of an artisan's hand having crafted them. Nothing it would appear had been spared in fitting out the new office.

Prescott didn't react to Nico's raised eyebrow as he crossed to a nearby cabinet and took out two glasses. He poured a glass of brandy for both of them and handed one to Nico.

As he took the glass, Nico recognized the familiar twisted pattern on its stem. It was Baccarat glass, usually only seen in the dining rooms of European royalty and noble families. Prescott had an obvious taste for the finer things in life.

"So how was your sea voyage from Rome? I expect the Mediterranean Sea is a little easier to navigate now that Napoleon's navy are no longer giving our ships grief. I must confess, I have always wanted to see the eternal city for myself," said Prescott.

Nico nodded, reminding himself to have some advertisements placed in the London newspapers. With the sea route to Italy no longer blocked by the French navy, the flow of tourists to Rome was a lucrative business he should make an effort to capitalize upon.

At the first sip of the brandy, he recognized it as being of excellent quality. Prescott had clearly decided he could help himself to one of the brandy barrels from the de Luca ships. From the fine cut of Prescott's suit, it was obvious he had engaged the services of an expensive tailor. Nico knew the annual salaries he paid his senior staff both in Italy and abroad. And while Prescott as head of business in London was paid well above market rates, he was not paid enough to afford hand-made clothing from the drapers and tailors of Savile Row.

Someone had to be paying for Phillip Prescott's high standard of living. There was one obvious candidate for whom that person was, and Nico had a growing suspicion it was him.

One of his set tasks while he was in London was to undertake an audit of the books of account of the English operations. A close inspection of the office outgoings was now added to Nico's list. If Prescott was living the highlife at the expense of his employer he was in for a nasty shock. Lorenzo de Luca had ensured that all his sons were taught how to work the double ledgers. They also knew how to read them for errors and discrepancies.

Nico could also read people. His first impressions of Phillip Prescott were thus far not favorable.

"Good. I've had my first night's sleep on dry land and hope to have my land legs back within a day or two. The tenants from New Cavendish Street have been most accommodating. The younger Mrs. Collins spent some time today with me and we visited Fortnum and Mason's. She has graciously promised to help me to reacquaint myself with London. It's hard to believe how much the city has changed since I was last here," he replied, maintaining his mask of indifference.

Prescott leisurely took a seat behind his desk, leaving Nico alone to find his own seat on a burgundy leather couch. When Prescott lounged back in his chair and sipped his brandy, Nico felt his left hand close in a tight fist.

If there was one trait he detested in a man it was the cold self-assured cockiness that his business manager was currently displaying. The hint of arrogance hung in the air.

"Yes, I find both the Collins women to be fine examples of widowhood. Which is why I thought of them when you requested for me to arrange accommodation other than staying at a hotel," replied Prescott.

Nico looked Prescott in the eye as he sensed the opportunity to see if he could make him squirm. He would dearly love to bring the self-important man down a peg or two.

"Was it also your idea to organize the household servants?" replied Nico.

He had to give Prescott his dues, only the slightest of twitches appeared at the corner of his mouth at Nico's words. It was gone as soon as it came.

"Ah, I wondered how long it would take you to discover my small deception," replied Prescott with a chuckle.

Nico raised an eyebrow.

Prescott set his brandy glass down and rose from his chair. "They can only afford to maintain a small retinue of servants which I knew would not suffice for your needs. A series of unfortunate events have reduced their station in life, but they both come from excellent families. By hiring the servants for the duration of your stay, they are treated to the comforts of having help around the house. Since it is nearly Christmas my lord, I thought you would approve of a little Christian charity. If I have overreached my delegated authority I can dismiss the servants."

"Hai me," Nico muttered under his breath. Prescott had finally addressed him with some sort of respect, but he knew it was only to smooth Nico's ruffled feathers. Prescott had the perfect answer and Nico could not challenge it without appearing to be a curmudgeon.

Prescott frowned. "Pardon?"

"It means well done in Italian," Nico lied. He would never admit that Prescott had for a moment got the better of him

Nico settled back on the couch, he was enjoying himself. With five younger brothers, he was the master of the banter. It was amusing to watch Prescott preen himself as he strutted around the room. It was obvious he thought Nico a fool.

Nico sighed, feigning surrender.

"The servants can stay but let us agree that neither of us is to mention this conversation to my tenants. As ladies of quality I would not wish to embarrass them. You did the right thing in arranging the servants," Nico replied.

By the time he finally left the shipping offices two hours later Nico was sure he had the measure of Phillip Prescott. After downing a second glass of brandy, Prescott let his guard down. He dropped several not so subtle hints about the clubs of which he was a member, and the exalted circles in which he and his wife moved.

The long carriage ride back to New Cavendish Street had Nico making good use of the time. He furiously made notes in his small pocket book. Prescott may have thought he was dealing with a wealthy fool, but Nico was from a family of Italian merchants who had been trading throughout Europe and the Far East since Marco Polo in the thirteenth century. It would take more than a glass of brandy and a well-cut suit to blind a de Luca to the truth about money.

He was generous to a fault with his own money, but it was money he had earned through hard work. Lorenzo de Luca had made all his sons work both the shipping office books and the ships themselves well before they came of age. Nico's strong physique bore testament to the long hours spent during the Italian summer working to offload his father's ships at the port of Civitavecchia.

Upon arriving back home, he marched upstairs and into his bedroom. He threw his coat over a nearby chair. With hands held firm on hips he stared into the flames of the fire burning in the fire place. The warmth in the room did little to placate his foul mood.

He was angry with himself. Prescott had got under his skin and stirred Nico's temper. Few men did that on meeting him for the first time.

"Don't go jumping to conclusions about things. You may have just taken an instant dislike to the man. He has never given you cause to doubt him before," he said.

His words did little to calm his rage. He gritted his teeth. Until today Prescott had been merely a name on a letter sent every few months some eight hundred miles from London to Rome. The London operation had run smoothly under Prescott's stewardship for the past seven years.

His gaze slowly drifted from the golden glow of the fire up to the mantelpiece. The vase had been moved from the dressing table and placed on top of the mantelpiece. It was now filled with red, yellow and white roses. A card had been placed against the side of the vase. He hurried over and picked up the card.

> *Dear Nico,*
> *I thought you might like some color for your room. I hope*
> *they meet with your approval.*
> *Kindest regards*
> *Isabelle*

When he answered the knock, which soon came on his bedroom door, he found the sender of the roses standing outside in the hallway.

Isabelle appeared nervous, holding her hands softly together, but he was encouraged when she met his gaze.

"I heard you come in. I was wondering if you had partaken of supper. If not, would you like to join me?" she said.

There was an unspoken strength about her he had not noticed until now. The skittish young woman who had asked to go home early from their trip was nowhere to be seen. She had clearly regrouped this afternoon and decided to make an offer of friendship. He could not deny her.

"Actually, I haven't eaten since earlier today. My meeting went late and by the time it was finished I did not wish to stay. I would love to join you. Will your cook be able to prepare anything at this hour of the night?" he replied.

An enchanting smile appeared on her face.

"We don't need cook to give us supper, remember the hamper you bought this morning, it is still intact. Well mostly. Ann and I did eat a few of the Portuguese egg tarts, but we made sure to leave you two. I set things up in the drawing room at the end of the hall on the off chance that you might come home early," she replied.

He noted the sheepish look on her face as she spoke. The day had been awkward between them. It pleased him that Isabelle was making an effort to overcome the missteps of his first day or so in the house.

He followed her down the hallway and into the sitting room at the end. Isabelle closed the door behind them.

"Ann has retired for the evening, so it is just the two of us. I hope you don't mind," she said.

She ushered him over to a pair of rounded back couches which sat in a semi-circle in front of a comfortable warm fire.

In front of the couches on a low table were the contents of the hamper basket, some plates and a bottle of opened wine. It was a cozy and quite romantic setting.

Something tells me you would be a mistress of seduction if you were so tempted.

As Isabelle took a seat on one of the couches Nico suddenly remembered the roses and her note.

"Before we eat, may I say thank you for the flowers. They were a very thoughtful gesture. The red, white and yellow buds match my family colors. I trust that was the intent," he said.

Isabelle nodded.

"There is a flower seller a few streets from here. I was surprised to find the yellow roses, they tend to be scare this time of year," she replied.

Nico picked up the bottle of wine and filled two glasses. He handed one to Isabelle before taking a seat on the couch opposite to her. Taking a sip of the wine, he was pleasantly surprised to discover it was a smooth dolcetto.

"You have good taste in wine Bella. If you would like I could arrange for some wine to be sent over from the de Luca shipping offices tomorrow. There were quite a few bottles on board the ship on which I arrived. Now let us see what we have for supper shall we?"

Isabelle picked up a plate laden with a selection of small pies and pastries and offered it to Nico.

"I had cook put them in the oven for a few minutes to warm them up a little while ago. They should still be hot," she said.

He selected a small pie with a square of pastry on the top it and took a bite.

"Curry! I cannot remember the last time I had a curry pie," he exclaimed.

Isabelle chortled. "I was wondering about those ones. Ann and I couldn't decide what the little square of pastry meant."

He picked up another of the curry pies and handed it to her. As their fingers touched, Nico felt a frisson of lust seize him. He pulled his hand away slowly, stunned by the effect Isabelle had had upon him.

As soon as she bit down on the spicy sauce Isabelle's eyes lit up with surprise. Another wave of lust coursed through Nico's body.

Get a grip of yourself man.

His gaze settled to linger on her face. The glow from the fire-place showed Isabelle's beauty in a soft light. Her dark brown eyes were like staring into a mirror of his own. If fate ever put them together, he was certain that their children would have eyes the color of dark Andalusite.

The thought settled comfortably in his mind, and much as he tried to move it to the background it would not shift. There was something about Isabelle which held his attention. She was tempta-tion wrapped up in a beautiful body.

"So, did you manage to complete your business dealings today?" asked Isabelle.

He took another drink from his wine glass before setting it down on the table. As he gathered his thoughts he found himself unable to meet her gaze.

He was grateful for her words. While his heart was busy running off making plans for a life with a woman barely of his acquaintance Nico's mind had been left rummaging for safe banal topics of conversation.

"Yes, I visited our new shipping offices at Wapping Dock. I was most impressed with the work that has happened down at London Docks in the years since I was last in England. Though I expect with trade now reopening in Europe the docks will have to be expanded once more," he replied.

They fell into silence for a moment, then Isabelle cleared her throat. "I was wondering if you have time tomorrow for us to take another outing. I would like to put the last day or so behind us and be able to show you the sights of London," she said.

Isabelle sat with her untouched glass of wine in her hand, her posture stiff and unsure. Phillip Prescott's discussion about the Collins women earlier in the evening came to Nico's mind. What hold did he have over them to force them into hosting a stranger in their home over Christmas?

He sensed his visit to the house meant more than just a few extra servants. There was an anxiousness about Isabelle that spoke of a real fear of offending him.

He knew it would do no go to ask her outright about his concerns. She was nervous enough without him pressing her for answers. He had four weeks until he was due to leave London and during that time Nico was determined to uncover the mystery of Isabelle Collins.

"I would like nothing better than for you and me to spend the day in town. But on one condition," he replied.

He heard her draw in a breath and then hold it.

"If we go to any shops or restaurants you must allow me to spend freely on you. I have three sisters and since they are all now married I am not permitted to take them out and spoil them rotten. You Bella shall have to indulge my desires."

Isabelle took a sip of her wine.

"May I ask you a personal question?" she said.

"Yes."

She went quiet for a moment. "Speaking of being married. Am I to assume that there is a Contessa de Luca? I ask because you have not mentioned your wife and you are travelling alone. I beg your pardon if you think I am being forward in asking," she said.

Nico was surprised that it had taken this long for one of the Collins women to enquire as to his marital status. On the morning of his arrival he had caught Ann Collins examining his fingers for a wedding ring. She had dropped several hints about him having a wife, but he had not been in the right mood to discuss his private life with a stranger.

"No, I do not have a contessa. I had expected to be married last Autumn, but the lady in question had a change of heart. She realized she didn't love me. She now lives in Venice and is married to someone else," he replied.

He heard himself say the words yet felt no emotion over them. A month or so ago he would have found the conversation difficult, even refused point blank to discuss the matter of his broken heart.

Yet here he found himself ready to lay open his soul to Isabelle. To tell her of his secret yearning for the love of a woman. His deep desire to have not only a wife by his side, but someone who shared his passion for life.

"Oh. I am so sorry," she said.

Nico nodded his acceptance of her kindness, comforted by the notion that his heart had finally accepted that Alessandra was now in the past. He had drunk himself to the bottom of enough bottles of chianti over his former fiancée. Since she had moved on with her life, he should endeavor to do the same.

"My mother always said that if one didn't marry for love, what was the point in living. After my fiancée called off our betrothal, my father told me to go to London. It is where he found my mother, so I think he may be hoping that lightning strikes a second time for a de Luca bachelor," he said.

Nico watched Isabelle as he spoke. He caught the look of happiness on her face as she registered his lack of a wife, then the hurt at hearing he had until recently had a fiancée. When he mentioned that his father had sent him to London in the hope that he may find a wife, she stilled.

"So, your father is still alive?" she asked.

He pretended not to notice the sudden and obvious change in direction of their conversation.

"Yes. Longevity runs on his side of the family. My grandfather lived into his ninth decade," he replied.

"So, if you are a count, then what is your father? I had assumed that titles were passed down the generations the same as in England and that you had inherited yours from your late father?" she said.

"My father is the Duke of Lazio. It's an area not far from Rome. We have a family villa there, but mostly we live in the ducal palace in Rome, close to the Vatican. My father works closely with the Holy See. Under the laws of the Holly See my father can hand down his titles while he is still alive," he replied.

He shifted in his seat and leaning over made a slow effort at picking up a bunch of grapes from one of the plates on the table. He hoped that his actions were clear enough for Isabelle to understand. He had given up enough of his private life to her tonight, she should cease with her subtle interrogation.

She sat forward on her couch and picking up a knife began to slice a piece of cheddar cheese.

"I am looking forward to our outing tomorrow, hopefully the weather will be fine," she said.

Nico popped a grape into his mouth and nodded.

Chapter Nine

I sabelle fell backward onto her bed and threw her arms out to the side. All that food and wine had her feeling fit to burst. She would never need to eat again.

It was well after midnight when she and Nico finally surrendered the battle against the Fortnum and Mason hamper. Between them they had fought bravely, but the last two boxes of sweet treats remained unopened.

"I shall have to wear sackcloth if he continues to feed me like that," she groaned.

She looked up at the ceiling. It was late and she was tired, and a little tipsy. But excitement about the forthcoming day kept her mind from thinking of sleep.

"You must indulge my desires," she whispered.

If only Nico had an inkling of her private desires. Of what sitting alone in the drawing room with him had been like for her. How much the mere touch of his fingers on hers had been thrilling.

She had held herself as prim and proper as she could, all the while wanting to reach out and touch those luscious lips of his. She imagined him a great kisser. And it was only a short journey in her mind to wonder what sort of a lover he would be if she were ever granted the chance to lay with him.

With his bachelor status now confirmed she gave free reign to her wicked thoughts. His fiancée had been a fool to throw away a life with Nico. His stylish clothes did little to hide his magnificent muscular body. A body she ached to touch. To possess.

The first year of marriage had shown her the joy of the marital bed. Long after everything with Anthony had turned sour she had clung to the faint hope that he would return to her bed. But her bed had remained cold and empty of her husband.

With Nico now sleeping in the same house, only a few doors from her room, hope sparked to life. The promise of once more knowing the pleasure of a man's hands and lips on her naked body had Isabelle rolling over onto her side and clutching her arms to her chest.

Don't. For your own sanity Isabelle, do not indulge in this fantasy.

Her mind cleared from the wine haze and she closed her eyes. Dreams of wonderful exotic lovers were for those who read romance books. The heroes in Jane Austen's books could be relied upon to give their heroine a happy ending. But the author herself had never married, never know the truth of how hard marriage could be. Isabelle Collins knew that the real world was a different place.

She drifted off to sleep, her dreams filled with images of her and Nico walking arm in arm on a sun kissed Italian beach. A blue sky and bright sun were overhead. A short way ahead of them on the sand raced several small children. When the children stopped they turned and waved.

"Mamma. Papa come see the seashells!" they happily cried.

In his room Nico was having his own moment of indecision. Isabelle had caught his eye on the first day of his arrival. Now it would appear she had also captured his imagination.

The evening spent alone in her company had drawn out his softer side. The side he usually managed to keep well hidden from the rest of the world.

He shook his head. He was always falling in love, constantly searching for that one woman whose heart he could claim as his own. It was a burden being a true romantic.

"She is a widow and therefore not constrained by the usual dictates of society. An affair could be an agreeable arrangement," he said.

She knew he was not encumbered with a wife or family. A quiet intimate relationship between a bachelor and a respectable widow would be within the boundaries of propriety.

He wanted Isabelle.

Thoughts of his mother came to him as they often did at this hour. Elizabeth would be outraged at such a notion. She would never have allowed him to act in such a way with a vulnerable woman. Tempting though it was, he would never be able to look himself fully in the mirror again if he treated Isabelle as a short-term diversion in his bed.

There was no middle ground as far as he and Isabelle were concerned. Either they remained friends or they married. The idea of taking her for his wife was surprisingly appealing.

Chapter Ten

Isabelle's stomach grumbled in warning. It was well past two o'clock and she had not eaten since sharing the late supper with Nico. She tried silently explaining to her belly that it had been well and truly full when she went to bed, but her body wasn't interested. She was hungry.

Nico looked up from the Turkish rug he was standing on and as their gazes met he chuckled.

"Well the sooner you decide which one we are to buy, the sooner we can go and find food," he said.

They had been in the carpet shop for over an hour while Nico made the unfortunate shop owner haul out rug after rug for his perusal. Isabelle was seated on a pile of rolled up carpets to one side of the main display gallery.

"You do understand the difference between need and want?" she asked.

He raised an enquiring eyebrow. "Are you going to quote Adam Smith's Wealth of Nations to me? If so I shall have you know that I studied economics at Sapienza University in Rome," he replied.

"Oh. What degree did you earn?" she asked.

A wicked smile appeared on his face. One that she was beginning to gain an appreciation of from the time they had spent together.

"I didn't say I finished. There were too many ships in my father's fleet to manage. That and other distractions made me leave my studies," he replied.

He went back to examining the rug, leaving Isabelle to ponder what the other distractions could have been in young Nico's life. It didn't take long for her to come to the obvious conclusion. He was a divinely handsome man from an Italian noble family. Of course, many a pretty young sonorità would have found a way to tear him from his studies.

And yet you have never married.

"I think the dark red one will do," announced Nico.

Isabelle roused from her thoughts and gave a sigh of relief as Nico pointed to a rug he had examined five rugs earlier.

"And before you ask. Yes, I do need a rug in my room. And if you behave yourself I may just leave it behind when I go," he added.

She forced a smile to her lips at his words, but the truth was it hurt to hear him talking of leaving England. After the night they had spent alone in the sitting room she sensed her heart was already making up its mind to belong to him. When the new year came, so would heart break.

As the relieved shop owner went about the business of wrapping Nico's purchase, Nico himself continued to shuffle about on the other rug. When he caught her eye, Isabelle was gifted with an impromptu jig. She clapped her hands in delight.

"All those hours of tortuous dance lessons and this is all I have to show for it," he said.

"Please continue. It makes me feel so much better about my own inadequacies when it comes to dancing. Though I do enjoy the pleasures of the waltz," she replied.

Nico stopped, then started toward her. She felt a flush of heat race to her cheeks as he approached. He took hold of her hand and pulled her to her feet.

"Come show me how well you dance my Bella, remember you promised to indulge me," he said.

Holding her close Nico spun Isabelle into a waltz. He was as skilled as she knew he would be, a master of the dance. The sound of Isabelle's laughter rang through the shop as Nico lifted her up and spun her round. She let her head fall back, exalting in the bliss of pure enjoyment.

The smile was still wide on her face when the shop owner returned with the paperwork for the sale of the rug. Nico slowly lowered Isabelle back to her feet. He raised his eyebrow mischievously at her as he signed the invoice. Isabelle chuckled.

She put a tremulous hand to her chest. Her heart was racing at a fast gallop. She had never met a man who lived life as large as Count Nico de Luca. His home in Italy must surely be filled with merriment and joy.

"Are you ready to leave? We should go and find somewhere that serves a nice piece of fish. I used to dine at Simpson's Tavern over at Billingsgate but they foolishly don't allow ladies inside. Perhaps one of the small fish mongers in the street over from them will cook us a nice piece of haddock. We will have to eat it outside in the carriage, but that is no matter. What do you say?"

She nodded. It was only a piece of fish, but she felt like Nico was offering her the world. As he took her arm, Isabelle shyly looked away.

It was foolish and it would end in a broken heart, but she knew from bitter experience that love was a determined emotion. She was falling in love with Nico de Luca and there was nothing she could do.

Chapter Eleven

"I am surprised you were both able to fit into the carriage what with all the boxes and bags of shopping you brought home. And a rug?" said Ann, at breakfast the following morning.

"I didn't buy anything yesterday. It was all our guest's work in the shops. By the time we reached the end of Oxford Street word must have got out that a mad Italian nobleman was in town freely spending his money. When we arrived at the last shop, the owner almost tripped over his feet in his haste to open the door, it was very amusing," replied Isabelle.

"Well as long as you had fun, which from the laughter I heard when you arrived home you certainly did," replied Ann.

The door to the breakfast room opened and Nico stepped inside.

"Good morning ladies, may I join you?" he said.

Isabelle straightened her back and gave him a warm smile. Without thinking she tucked a wayward curl behind her ear. Across the table from her Ann picked up her cup of coffee and smiled.

Isabelle was flirting.

Nico gathered up a plate from the main table and wandered over to the platters of warm food which were on a side table.

"Ah salmon. Cook did get my note about fish at breakfast excellent," he said, picking up a piece of baked fish and dropping it onto his plate.

Isabelle and Ann exchanged a look. Fish for breakfast was well outside their financial means. Ann had several unkind words to say about their guest when she informed Isabelle that the standard eggs and toast were not going to meet with Nico's exacting requirements.

Nico took a seat at the end of the table and tucked heartily into his food.

"Do you have plans for today in town?" asked Ann.

He finished his mouthful. "Actually, I am leaving town later this afternoon. I am headed to my uncle's estate in Chobham. Perhaps you know the place since it is also in Surrey," he replied.

Isabelle's blood froze. The lie about the Collins family estate was suddenly on shaky ground.

"Ah yes. I have heard of Chobham, though it is situated at the more northerly part of the county than us," replied Ann, without blinking.

There was a moment of silence in the room, punctuated only by the sound of Nico putting down his knife and fork.

"I was thinking that perhaps you ladies would like to join me. I will only be staying with my mother's family for a few days, after which we would be free to visit your home. You could check on things since all the staff are now here in London," he said.

Isabelle sat waiting for the axe to fall. Surrey wasn't so large a county that Ann could miraculously invent a town and hope that Nico didn't press them into visiting it with him.

"Thank you for the kind offer, but I have much to do in London before Christmas. Besides, the servants have just got settled in here, it would make no sense for us to make them all move back again," replied Ann.

Well played. Isabelle fought the temptation to clap in appreciation of Ann's clever retort.

"Well then. Perhaps Isabelle could be spared. She could accompany me. Would you like to see my English ancestral home Bella?" he asked.

When their gazes met he smiled at her. Isabelle was caught between the fear of having her lie exposed and her aching desire to be with Nico. Time spent travelling together in the coach would be precious time alone with him. Her head and heart were locked in battle.

"What a lovely offer. I think that would be wonderful don't you my dear? You could visit with Nico's relatives and then return to London in time to assist me with Christmas preparations," said Ann.

Isabelle's gaze drifted from Nico to Ann. Out of the corner of her eye she could see he was watching her every move. Had he remembered her false step over mentioning where their fictious estate was based?

"But don't you need me to stay in London?" she replied, through gritted teeth.

"Nonsense. I can manage it on my own. You go and enjoy yourself in the country. It will do you the world of good to get out of the misery that is London."

Nico wiped his face with his napkin and rose from the table.

"Excellent. Then it is settled. Isabelle you shall accompany me to visit my family in Chobham. I am sure you will find Higham Place to your liking," he said.

Once he was gone, Isabelle dismissed the servants. Panic gripped her.

"Why did you do that?" she asked.

Much as she wanted to spend time alone with Nico, she was now faced with the prospect of having to maintain the lie of their circumstances. Leaving London and meeting Nico's English family in the countryside was the last thing she wished to do. They would tear through her lie in an instant.

"I did it because getting out of London will do you good. And it will help to push things along with the two of you," replied Ann.

Isabelle's mouth opened, denial on her lips but the raising of Ann's eyebrow stopped her before she could speak. Ann pointed toward the door through which Nico had recently departed.

"Count de Luca is the greatest prize the Roman gods could have sent us. An unwed, wealthy nobleman. He has so much more to offer you than some staid English gentleman. So, if you think for one minute I am going to stand by and let you dilly and dally about snatching him up for yourself you are seriously mistaken. Let us finish our breakfast and get your travel wardrobe assembled. You are going to Surrey!"

By three o'clock the area out the front of the house was a hive of activity. Boxes and bags were being loaded on the top of the travel coach which Nico had hired for the trip to Surrey.

Isabelle and Ann moved to one side as Nico came out of the house carrying the tall thin box he had brought with him on the first day. Instead of handing it up to the staff to put on the roof, he placed inside the coach.

"I wonder what is in that box. It must be precious if he does not trust the servants to handle it," observed Ann.

Isabelle looked down at the small travel case in her hand. Her mind was too busy coming up with all manner of terrible outcomes from the journey ahead to pay any attention to the box.

A gentle hand touched her face, and she looked up at her mother in law.

"Take a chance on this man. If you feel the moment is right then tell him the truth of our circumstances. I would not be surprised if he had already drawn his own conclusions about the servants."

She looked past Ann to where Nico was standing talking to the head driver of the coach. There was a lot of nodding from the driver. When the driver pulled his pocket watch out and checked it, Isabelle sensed it was time for her to take her leave.

"I had better get on board," she said.

Ann leaned in and kissed her cheek. "Good luck," she whispered.

Nico took hold of Isabelle's hand and helped her up into the coach. A nearby servant handed Isabelle a woolen blanket, which she placed over her knees. The coach while well-appointed was still only made of wood and offered little protection from the winter elements.

"Time to go," announced Nico. With a nod of his head toward Ann, he climbed aboard the coach and pulled the door shut.

"We should be at Higham Place by supper time. The road out from London is well provisioned with coaching inns so changing the horses should not present a problem," he said, taking his seat on the bench opposite to Isabelle.

As the coach pulled into the street, Isabelle returned Ann's wave of goodbye. Ann stood for a moment out the front of the house. Isabelle knew it was to make certain that she did not have a change of heart and attempt to cry off on the trip.

"Mrs. Collins will be fine while you and I are out of town. I have given her private use of my town carriage," he said.

"Yes, that was very generous of you," replied Isabelle. She knew Ann well enough to know that she would have the carriage brought around to the front of the house as soon as Isabelle and Nico were out of sight.

A little while after the travel coach made the turn onto the Tyburn turnpike, Nico pulled a small box out of his coat pocket.

"We de Luca's always give gifts when we apologize," he said.

Isabelle looked at the small blue box as Nico held it out to her. Why was he apologizing?

"A small confession. I wanted you to come with me to Higham Place, because I want us to spend some time together. To get to know one another a little more. I am apologizing because you were pressured by both Ann and myself into coming," he said.

She took the box from his hands and opened it. Inside was a pair of silver earrings with sapphire drops. Isabelle closed the box and handed it promptly back.

"You don't need to give me things just because you feel you need to apologize. I don't need things," she said.

He took the box with obvious reluctance. From the look on his face people didn't normally refuse his expensive gifts. Isabelle was in love and she was going to hold fast. She would not be bought.

"What can I give you?" he asked.

"Yourself. If you want to know the real me. Relationships, whether friendships or otherwise are formed through connection," she replied.

He rose from his seat and came to sit beside her. Taking her hand in his he lifted it to his lips. The soft warmth of his lips on her fingers sent chills down her spine. Another step in her heated imagining of this man was coming true.

"Will you allow me to kiss you? I have wanted to since the moment we met," he asked.

Allow? She was all but begging him to kiss her.

When she nodded, Nico leaned in and cupped her face in his hands. The first kiss when their lips met was barely a touch. Soft, hesitant, seeking permission. He pulled away briefly but returned when Isabelle whispered. "Nico."

The second kiss held greater promise. As he claimed her mouth she opened her lips and let his tongue sweep inside. She grabbed a hold of the lapel of his coat and pulled him toward her.

Their lips tangled in a slow sensual dance. Her nipples hardened against the fabric of her gown. Her body slowly awakening from its long slumber of husbandly neglect and widowhood stirred into life. Desire flared.

Nico slid a hand around Isabelle's waist and held her firmly in place. She leaned back against his arm as he rose over her. The kiss deepened. When she heard the deep growl of need from him, a soft throb began to pulse between her legs. To be held by a man and kissed the way Nico was kissing her was a dark craving she had not dared to consider until now.

The coach hit a bumpy patch in the road, forcing them to break the kiss. As Nico pulled away, Isabelle caught the look of passion which burned in his eyes. There was no doubt he wanted her.

"Will you take the earrings now?" he said.

Isabelle shook her head. One passionate kiss was never going to meet the price of her heart.

"No. Keep your pretty things. The earrings are beautiful, but I want more. If trinkets are all that you want to offer to me, then perhaps we should let things be. Put the kiss down to nothing more than a moment of ill-thought pleasure between friends," she replied.

For a moment she understood the thrill of the gambler's soul. Risking a small hand for the chance of winning a bigger one. But she would not offer up her heart to a man who cared little for it. Cards had been Anthony's mistress, lies and sweet words his currency to buy Isabelle's affections. As she saw the look of uncertainty which now crossed Nico's face, she prayed that he didn't think to simply buy her heart.

"You are not like the other women I have known, and that is a good thing Isabelle Collins," he replied.

They changed horses at Sunbury-on-Thames, having spent the time since the kiss in nearly total silence. Isabelle had retrieved a book from her travel bag and sat reading. She did not look across to Nico for several hours.

His mind was too concerned with what to do about the beautiful widow seated opposite to attempt such a mundane pursuit as reading. He couldn't concentrate on anything other than how pleasurable holding her in his arms had been. How much he wanted to kiss her again.

He was a master in the art of seduction. He had kissed dozens of women in his time yet nothing came close to how he felt holding Isabelle.

Watching her as she sat with her nose in a book, an understanding slowly dawned on him. He had spent his adult life trying to buy love. He had spent a fortune on jewels and gowns in an attempt to win Alessandra's heart. Yet she too had handed all his gifts back when she found true love with another.

The coach slowed and turned onto a side road. Nico glanced at the wooden box standing on the floor next to him. Putting aside the matter of their relationship and its exact status, he knew he owed it to Isabelle to explain the true reason for his journey to Higham Place.

"We are making excellent time, we should arrive just after dusk," he said.

She looked up from her book.

"That's good news," she replied.

Her gaze fell on his arm which was resting on top of the wooden box. He looked down at the box.

"About the box," he ventured.

"Yes."

His hand instinctively went to his pocket, fingers touching on the small jewel box. Until today it had never occurred to him how much he used gifts to smooth his way with people. Isabelle would not take the earrings. He would have to offer up a naked apology.

He drew in a deep breath, suddenly unsure of himself.

"The trip to my uncle's house is the final stage of my mother's funeral. We are taking a portrait of her to be hung in the Higham family home. It was one of her last requests. She wanted something of herself to come home to England. I should have mentioned that before we set out, but I wasn't sure you would come if I told you," he said.

She closed the book and set it down on the bench beside her. Her countenance changed from one of indifference to sadness. Nico hated himself for having kept the truth from her.

"I wondered what the box was for when you first arrived. I figured it was something precious as you were angry with the coachman for dropping it. And when we left London earlier you would not let any of the staff handle it," she replied.

"Bella."

She sat forward and took hold of his hands.

"For all your wealth and power Nico de Luca, you are rather clueless when it comes to women. Why didn't you just ask me? If anyone understands the need for a friend during this time in their life it is me. If you had asked I would have said yes. You didn't need to try and pretend this trip was anything else. And before you go trying to offer me any more gifts, I am not angry with you, I am just hurt," she said.

She let go of his hands and sat back in her seat. His heart sank when she wiped away a tear. His offered handkerchief was politely refused. It had been a mistake to kiss her before he had explained the reason for their trip to Surrey. He was going to have to rethink his whole approach when it came to Isabelle.

"So, who exactly is in residence at Higham Place? I should at least be aware of whom I am going to meet," she said.

"My uncle is Sir Richard Higham who along with my aunt Eugenie are the current owners of Higham Place. My father was a guest at the estate many years ago. It is where he and my mother met," he replied.

"I see. So, what was an Italian nobleman doing in Surrey?" she asked.

He smiled. She had caught him in the long standing lie of how his parents had met. Few people ever queried the story, yet Isabelle had had the good sense to ask the obvious.

"When I say he met her at Higham Place, what I really meant was that my grandfather caught him climbing in through her bedroom window. My parents had been conducting a secret liaison in London during the summer and my father followed my mother home in order to steal her away to Italy," he replied.

'Your mother must have been a very special woman to have captured his heart. There must have been a thousand suitable women in Rome from which your father could have chosen his bride. Instead he chose her."

His hand patted the top of the box. He ached to see the portrait of his mother one last time. To know that at least the likeness of her had been safely returned home.

"No woman ever came close to Elizabeth Higham in my father's eyes. When you see her portrait, I think you will understand."

He softly chortled. He finally understood why his father had risked his neck in scaling the walls of Higham Place. Isabelle now held the same powerful hold over him.

Chapter Twelve

The coach drew to a halt just as the sun was setting. Isabelle put her face to the window and peered out. A series of torches set around the top of the drive lit up the front of the house.

Higham Place was a compact Queen Anne period home. Sandstone colored brickwork with white painted windows. A simple set of stairs led up to the front door of the house. Matching wings with three sets of windows ran either side of the front entrance. It had a homely feel which made Isabelle fall in love with it at first sight.

Before they alighted from the coach, household servants quickly assembled in a long line to the front steps. At the top of the steps stood a man and woman.

"Your aunt and uncle?" asked Isabelle.

A soft grin appeared on Nico's face, along with tears which shone in his eyes. His obvious affection for his family needed no words.

As she stepped down from the coach Nico took Isabelle by the hand. Lord and Lady Higham greeted them at the bottom of the steps.

"Nico! How wonderful," exclaimed Lady Higham, as Nico wrapped his arms around her. They held one another for some time.

Lord Higham bowed low to Isabelle.

"Richard Higham at your service."

She held out a hand. "Isabelle Collins. I am a friend of your nephew."

Over the past hour or so she had sat and pondered the question of what she was to say to Nico's relatives. It didn't seem right to announce that she was merely his tenant. It was not customary for landlords to take their tenants on trips to country. In the end she decided to let Nico do the explaining. It had been his idea to bring her along, so it was up to him as to what he wished to tell his aunt and uncle.

"Nicholas. It is good to see you. Pity it took these circumstances for you to come back to England," said Lord Higham, hugging his nephew.

Nico looked across to Isabelle.

"My full name is Nicholas. My mother chose it, but my father made certain that I was addressed as Nico from the day I was born," he explained.

Isabelle tucked that piece of information away in her mind, intending to call him Nicholas the next time he stepped out of line.

Once inside, Lady Higham showed her to her room.

"I'm sorry we were not aware that Nico was bringing a friend, so please excuse the chill in the room the fire has only just been lit," said Lady Higham.

Isabelle put her travel bag down. "My coming was very last minute. Thank you for welcoming me into your home Lady Higham," she said.

A smiling Lady Higham took hold of Isabelle's hand.

"Please call me Eugenie. I hope this will not be your last trip to Higham Place. Just ring the bell if you are in need of anything. Supper will be shortly, do come down to join us," she said.

When Isabelle came down to supper a short time later, Nico was waiting for her at the bottom of the staircase. He offered his arm, which she shyly took.

"I have spoken to my uncle and he has made arrangements for the service tomorrow. I know you do not wish to be away from London for too long, so we shall remain here for only a few days. I hope in the meantime that you will grant me the opportunity to show you the grounds. This is my favorite place in England," he said.

She sensed a calm in Nico's demeanor she had not noted before in their short acquaintance. If she had to put a word to it, she would have said he was happy.

"I like your family. They are nice people. Your aunt said she hoped this would not be my last visit to Higham Place. I hope so too," she replied.

He stopped. Their gazes met. As his deep brown eyes searched hers, she knew he was seeking permission once more from her. Her agreement to use the time away from London to decide on the next steps in their relationship.

"My mother returned home to England on a regular basis. Italy is only a few weeks away by boat," he replied.

Her chest tightened. Until this moment she had never seriously contemplated that her future might lie in another country. That if she was to be with Nico, it may mean giving up her homeland.

"I suppose there is that, but who knows what the future holds," she said.

She had given up much to seek a future with Anthony and it had ended with her life in shattered pieces. If she and Nico were to move forward with their relationship it would have to be with carefully considered steps.

Chapter Thirteen

"Did you sleep well?"

Nico was standing on the landing of the house's grand staircase when Isabelle came down the next morning.

She found herself nodding at Nico despite the reality of her sleepless night. After returning to her room following a late supper she had sat and stared into the fire. She chided herself for being foolish enough to fall in love with him. They were barely past the point of being strangers, yet Nico was already talking about how easy it would be for her to travel back to England for visits home.

"The beds here are very comfortable. Your aunt and uncle have a lovely home," she replied.

He drew close.

"Will you walk with me this morning? A stroll before breakfast always helps to build a hearty appetite," he said.

There was undisguised lust and desire in his words. He was not talking about food. She swallowed deep. Temptation beckoned.

"Yes, that would be lovely, country air is such a refreshing change after London," she replied.

Once outside, Nico wasted no time in getting Isabelle away from the house and inner gardens. With almost indecent haste he had steered her up a nearby path and into a grove of trees opposite the main drive.

As soon as they were out of sight of the house, he pulled her roughly to him.

"Bella," he murmured, as his head lowered.

She knew she should fight against wanting him. Against offering up all she had, but as soon as his lips touched her, defeat was inevitable.

As his tongue swept into her mouth she met him fully within the kiss. His fingers fumbled with the opening of her cloak, then set to her buttons. Isabelle made no effort to stop him.

When the chill of the morning air kissed her naked skin, she closed her eyes. His lips left her mouth and trailed down her neck. Butterfly kisses interspersed with soft whispers of love.

"Bella," he moaned, as he took her breast in his hand and ran his fingers over her puckered nipple. Heat pooled in her loins. She speared her fingers into his hair, inviting him to linger and play. When he rolled her nipple between his fingers, she whimpered.

She was caught up in the moment, ready to do his bidding. Willing to give him everything.

Everything but the truth.

The thought pulled her up sharp.

"Stop. Please stop," she cried.

Nico let go and stepped away. Isabelle quickly covered herself and set her gown to right.

"I cannot. I cannot do this to you," she stammered.

He huffed in disappointment. "From what I recall, it was me doing something to you."

"I mean. I can't be intimate with you when I am not being truthful. We don't have an estate in Surrey," she said.

He chuckled. "Or Wiltshire. I did think you were not telling me the truth from that first day. If Prescott had not confirmed it, then the fact that your so-called servants do not know where anything is in your house should have been a very large clue to your lie."

Isabelle stood opened mouthed with shock. Nico knew. He had known all along. It didn't make sense. Prescott had been at great pains to ensure that she and Ann had stayed silent on their arrangement, yet he had obviously told Nico.

"So, you also know about the rental agreement?" she ventured.

The lightness of his mood disappeared, and Isabelle immediately wished she had kept her mouth shut.

"What rental agreement?" he replied.

She drew in a shaky breath. Prescott had not told Nico about the rent. She cursed herself for her stupidity, all the while wondering how much damage she had already done to their fragile relationship.

The truth was the only way forward.

"Prescott offered us six months free rent if we hosted you during your stay in London. Ann and I are hoping to use the money we save in rent to launch me back into society," she replied.

"So, you can find yourself a new husband?" he replied. She heard the jealousy in his voice as he spoke.

"Please. I don't want to get Mr. Prescott into any trouble. He was very gracious when he came to inform us that Anthony had sold you the house. He even sat with us when Anthony went missing in Brighton; and reassured us that we would have first choice on the house as tenants when Anthony's body was finally located," she said.

Nico's mouth opened in a small 'o' and Isabelle was certain he was about to speak again, but for some unknown reason he stopped himself. He motioned for her to continue.

"I don't like lying to people. It's just that the offer to host you was too good to refuse. And truth be told I thought you would be a much older, married gentleman."

He fixed his gaze on her, his look wary.

"And why would that make a difference?" he asked.

Isabelle closed her eyes. The last thing she wanted to do at this moment was tell Nico how she truly felt about him. She had just confessed to two lies, who was to say he wouldn't think her words to be yet another fabrication.

But she was caught in the moment.

"Because if you were an older, married man I would still feel badly about lying to you. But my soul would not tear into a thousand pieces every time I looked into your eyes."

"Bella," he growled.

His arms were around her in an instant, pulling her into his embrace. She slipped her arms around his waist, holding on tight. She feared to let go.

He kissed her hair and murmured. "I will give you a life time of free rent Bella, you only have to ask."

She looked up at him as hope sparked in her heart.

"You are not angry? I have been lying to you all this time, how can you not be?"

He lowered his head and captured her lips in a long, slow kiss. His fingers set to work on the bodice of her gown once more.

The sound of a horse and carriage clattering on the stone flagging of the drive had them both looking back to the house. Lord Higham and a second gentleman alighted from a carriage. Nico sighed. "The local minister. He is going to conduct the service for my mother. I had better go and greet him," he explained.

The family had arranged for the local vicar to conduct a short service in the family chapel before the unveiling of Elizabeth de Luca's portrait on the main staircase of the house.

Isabelle was glad of the sudden interruption. She needed time alone to think. The past few minutes had shaken her composure.

"I am going to go for a short walk. I need time to think before seeing your family again," she said.

Nico held out his hand, a worried look now sat on his face.

"You will come to the service?"

She followed his gaze as it settled on the small stone chapel which stood to one side of the main house. Lord Higham and the vicar were headed toward its front door.

"Of course," she replied.

Isabelle watched as Nico walked back down the path and crossed over to the stone chapel.

"I love you," she whispered.

Chapter Fourteen

I sabelle had hoped to stand at the back of the chapel and leave the service to the Higham family, but Nico had other ideas. As soon as she stepped outside the house later that afternoon, he was waiting. With a smile he took her arm.

"You look beautiful, my mother would approve," he said, looking at her pale green gown.

She blushed. The gown was an old one that Ann and she had worked on to repurpose. The plain white buttons which ran down the back had been replaced with silver ones and a matching silver underskirt. The changes added color and interest to the gown. She was particularly proud of her needlework on the underskirt.

"Thank you," she replied.

Inside the chapel the family and estate servants gathered along with a few older members of the local gentry. While Elizabeth had left England many years before, she was still a member of the Higham community. People had come to pay their respects.

Nico escorted Isabelle to the front pew where they took their places alongside his aunt and uncle. Isabelle shyly smiled at Lord Higham as Nico handed her a hymn book and they sat down.

As the minister began the short service, Isabelle sat with her hands folded softly in her lap. She glanced over at Nico. His left hand was fisted tightly on his knee. His jaw was set hard and he was slowly grinding his teeth.

She turned her head and looked forward, too ashamed to look at him any longer. While she had suddenly taken it upon herself to confess all her secrets, she had quite forgotten that Nico was about to say his final goodbyes to his mother.

Selfish. Self-centered. How could you do that Isabelle.

The memorial service was mercifully short. A few kind words were said by an old childhood friend of Elizabeth, followed by some pleasant hymns. As services went it was nicer than any funeral Isabelle had attended.

"Simple and quick, the best kind of funeral services," said Nico as they stepped out into the afternoon sunshine. He took hold of her hand and raised it to his lips.

"My mother's funeral in Rome went on for two days, I was utterly exhausted by the end of it. My sisters had all cried themselves out, and my father was shattered. Today, it was refreshing to have a simple English service. Of course, it did help that there was not a burial to manage this time," he said.

Their gazes met and she saw sadness in his eyes. She had lost someone, the same as he had, but that was where all similarities ended. She had hated Anthony by the end. Her bitter grief had been for all the wasted years he had stolen from her. Of promises made but never kept.

Nico was living the grief of someone who had lost a part of themselves. It was so tangible that she could almost touch it.

"Come on, let us go inside and see her portrait. I want to see my mother back in her old home," he said.

The portrait unveiling was a private family affair. Just Lord and Lady Higham, Nico and Isabelle. No one seemed to find it odd that someone who had never known Elizabeth was present at her final farewell.

Lord Higham stood silently in front of the shrouded portrait on the first landing of the staircase. Nico and Isabelle stood together facing the painting of an older gentleman which hung on the wall opposite.

"That's my grandfather," he said, pointing to the painting.

Tears sprang to Isabelle's eyes at his words. It was a touching gesture on the part of Nico's uncle. Father and daughter would forever be able to see each other from where their portraits hung.

Lord Higham lifted the black cloth which covered the portrait and Isabelle got her first look at the late Duchess of Lazio.

She immediately understood why Lorenzo de Luca had risked his neck to climb in through the bedroom window at Higham Place. The woman he had wooed and wed was a stunning English beauty. Her brown eyes were the same as her son, warm pools of kindness.

Beside her Nico stiffened and sucked in a deep breath.

"God, I miss her," he whispered.

Isabelle slipped her hand into his and softly squeezed. He looked at her, words were not needed. Her presence beside him meant more than just a friend giving support. By taking his hand Isabelle was making a statement to the world in front of Nico's family.

"Thank you for bringing my sister home Nico. Our Elizabeth is home once more," said Lord Higham.

Lady Higham closed her eyes before bringing a hand to cover her face. She quietly sobbed. Nico looked to Isabelle, who released his hand and stepped back allowing him to give comfort to his grieving aunt.

Isabelle held out a hand to Lord Higham.

"I am so sorry Richard," she said.

He looked at his sister's portrait and drew Isabelle in to stand beside him. They faced the portrait of Elizabeth.

"She would approve of you. With an English wife Nico will have to keep returning here. The connection will be forged anew with you Isabelle. It is exactly what she would have wanted," he said.

"What she would have wanted is for us to have champagne. I promised my mother only a few tears would be shed when I brought her home, and I intend to keep to my word," said Nico.

A servant appeared bearing a tray of champagne glasses. Lord Higham wiped the tears from his eye and smiled. Nico took two glasses and handed one each to his aunt and uncle. Then he handed one to Isabelle.

"My family doesn't do funerals like others. We grieve, but we also celebrate. My mother had a wonderful life. She lived and she loved. Let us raise a glass to her," said Nico.

The four of them raised their glasses to Elizabeth's portrait.

"Welcome home. Benvenuto a casa," said Nico before emptying his glass.

"It is beautiful here," said Isabelle.

She and Lady Higham were taking a turn about the garden in the early evening. Lady Higham pointed toward a wooded glade. "Elizabeth and my husband used to play hide and seek in there when they were children. It is where Nico used to come and sit whenever he arrived on term-break from school."

"He has not spoken much of his time in England, but I gather from the little he has said that his school days here were not happy times," replied Isabelle.

Lady Higham nodded.

"Yes, the boys at school did not care that Nico was the son of a duke. They considered him to be a dirty foreigner with ties to the Catholic church. Every term-break he would come to us, his body covered in bruises and his clothes in tatters. He would spend hours walking the grounds of the estate trying to burn off his rage. Then he would pack up the new clothes we bought him and go straight back to school. He hated it here but he came back every year for five years just to please his mother," she said.

Isabelle looked back toward the house. Nico and his uncle were standing on the balcony outside. Nico waved to her. She shyly waved back.

"But why did he continue to come here if he hated it so much?"

Tears sprang to Lady Higham's eyes and her bottom lip trembled. "Because if you knew Elizabeth you would know that Nico could not refuse her anything. I thought she had insisted he return here because she wished for her first-born son to be an English gentleman. It was only after Richard and I visited the family in Rome that we discovered she was completely unaware of how terrible a time he was having at school in England. It broke her heart."

Isabelle sighed. It must have been hard for Nico all those years to conceal the truth from his mother. Yet so great was his love for her that every year he got back on board a ship and returned to school in England.

"It does explain his reluctance to remain here any longer than is absolutely necessary," replied Isabelle.

It also explained why none of his younger brothers had been sent to school in England. Through his own suffering Nico had saved his siblings from a similar fate. Even from having known him for a short time, she was not surprised at his self-sacrifice.

"And what about you Isabelle? What are you going to do when Nico gets on board that boat and goes home, will you go with him?" asked Lady Higham.

Isabelle bit down on her lip. Until today she had not faced her true feelings for Nico. Her mind was still caught up in hurried kisses and revelations.

"I don't honestly know. Matters between us have not reached near to a point for discussion of a possible future together," she replied. Lady Higham raised an eyebrow but let Isabelle's words alone.

❦

On the balcony Nico and his uncle watched the women walk the grounds.

"She is a true beauty," remarked Lord Higham.

Nico nodded. He couldn't take his eyes off Isabelle. It was as if he feared that she would walk into the woods and never return.

He knew it was his mind still coming to terms with the loss of one woman. After their encounter in the wood earlier that morning, he was determined to press ahead and secure Isabelle's position in his life. To make her his contessa.

"But there is something else on your mind, I can tell you are troubled," said Lord Higham.

Isabelle's confession about Phillip Prescott was a splinter in Nico's mind he could not move. She had been sworn to secrecy and that did not speak well for Prescott's so called professed charitable motives.

"I need someone to investigate my London based man of business. Several things have transpired since my arrival to give me cause to think he may not be honest in his dealings with the de Luca family business and our money," he replied.

Lord Higham cleared his throat. "How deep do you wish this investigation to go? There are chaps who will give a once-over look at him and let you know what they think. On the other hand, I have at my disposal a certain gentleman with a particular set of skills who could go as deep as you wish," he said.

At this juncture Nico had little to go on. Other than the generous offer of free rent to Isabelle and an obvious taste for the finer things in life, Prescott hadn't actually done anything wrong. A light touch was still in order.

"Perhaps I could dig into things a little myself and then if I uncover anything which appears out of sorts, I could call on your man," replied Nico.

He would have to tread softly when it came to investigating Phillip Prescott. Isabelle had a good opinion of the man. If Nico made unfounded accusations against him, Isabelle would not be happy.

Her words from earlier that morning sat in the forefront of his thoughts.

Anthony had sold you the house.

Prescott had been very clear in his correspondence to Nico. The house at New Cavendish Street had been a deceased estate. The previous owner's widow and mother were a mere footnote to the investment.

Something was not right. Either Isabelle was mistaken in her understanding, or Prescott was lying.

"That sounds like a sensible plan. I shall give you the name and details of my contact before you and Isabelle leave tomorrow," his uncle replied.

Isabelle and Lady Higham began to make their way back toward the house. Lord Higham smiled lovingly at his wife.

He turned to Nico. "So, is history about to repeat itself? Is England going to lose yet another of its rare beauties to the charms of a de Luca male?"

Nico chuckled. "I am working on it."

Lord Higham gave him a friendly pat on the shoulder. "Well considering that your aunt has already chosen the names of your first five children you had better get a wriggle on and seal the deal with that young woman. A beauty like Isabelle will not stay a widow for very long once she is officially back on the marriage market."

His uncle was right. Even in her widow's weeds Isabelle would make a man look twice. As soon as other eligible gentlemen got wind that a diamond of the first water such as Isabelle Collins was seeking a new husband they would be falling over themselves to court her. Nico would be crushed in the stampede.

Time was of the essence. If he was going to convince Isabelle that her future lay in being his wife he could not delay.

"I shall speak to her as soon as I can. As she will need time to consider such a major change in her life I would be a fool to delay."

"Good lad. Your parents would be proud."

Lord Higham left Nico alone on the balcony. He stood enjoying the afternoon sunshine for a time, there was little warmth in the air but it was still better than being in grimy London. The Surrey air was sweet and clean.

The thought of Isabelle and what he would say to her now occupied his mind. She had been honest with him, and in doing so he had watched the weight of the world lift off her shoulders. With no secrets to keep them apart, they could turn their attention to exploring what did lay between them.

Chapter Fifteen

I sabelle attended supper, but it was very much a family affair. Nico, Richard, and Eugenie each had their own stories to tell of Elizabeth. After an hour or so Isabelle sensed she was intruding on their privacy.

"I might turn in early if you please excuse me. It's been a long day and the three of you should have some time together without a stranger in the room," she said.

Nico stood and offered her his arm. He walked her to the door and out into the hallway.

"I didn't mean for this evening to be all about my mother. It was rude of me to shut you out," he said.

Isabelle lifted a hand to his face, brushing her fingers tenderly along the stubble of his early evening beard.

"Today should be about your mother. A part of her has come home. Home to her family. Your aunt and uncle grieve for her. It does them both good for you to be here. I've watched their faces light up whenever you mention Elizabeth. For them you are her. Please go and spend time with them."

He bent down and kissed her. Isabelle offered up her lips, love and tenderness for this man warmed her heart.

"I shall go and read in the library for a while then turn in for bed," she said.

§

When the clock in the hallway struck eleven Isabelle rose from her chair and put down the book she had been unsuccessfully attempting to read for the past two hours. Memories of the moment when she held hands with Nico concentrated her mind. It was the moment when she finally allowed her heart to speak its mind. She was in love with him.

He had been honest with her about Alessandra, sharing his deepest thoughts, yet she still held back her own truth from him.

She stopped outside Nico's bedroom, surprised to find his door open. In the doorway she caught sight of him, seated on a small couch, a glass of whisky in his hand. She knocked gently on the door.

"May I speak with you?" she asked.

He rose from his seat, a soft smile on his lips. He bowed.

"Please do come in. I am sure there are no servants about the upper floors at this time of night, so there will be no need to concern yourself with being seen."

Isabelle stepped into the room, closing the door quietly behind her. She was a widow and while it was socially acceptable for widows to have private liaisons she had never thought to find herself alone in a man's bedroom. A man who was not her husband.

"Could I offer you a nightcap? I am sure there is some sweet port in the cabinet," he said.

She nodded. A nip of alcohol would hopefully calm her nerves. She was no wedding night virgin but being alone with Nico in his room was still making her heart race.

"Thank you," she said, taking a glass of the dark rose wine. He moved along on the couch and made room for her to sit beside him. She glanced at an empty chair nearby but counselled herself. She was here to speak her heart to him, now was not the time to keep her distance from him.

"I missed you this evening. I'm sorry if my family and I got a little too involved with stories of my mother," he said.

"No, it is I who should apologize. Today was a day to remember your mother, I should have stayed and listened."

He scowled. Then reached out and took hold of her hand.

"Then let us forgive one another and talk of other things. There is still the matter of unfinished business from this morning. I want to know how far you were willing to let me go," he said.

His voice was edged with gruff desire. Temptation and all its glory beckoned, yet something held her back. What if she did confess her love to him, and it was not reciprocated? From the few moments of tenderness between them she was unsure of his true feelings for her.

Perhaps Nico saw her as a comfortable option for a wife. Someone who would be grateful for having been rescued from a life of near penury. A beautiful English woman who would meet with his family's approval. A woman whose portrait would one day also grace the walls of Higham Place.

She stood up and set the glass of port down. This was a foolish mistake. For the second time in her life she was on the verge of offering up her heart to a man, and once again she could not be sure that he understood its true value.

"Bella, what's wrong?" he asked, getting to his feet.

"I should not have come to your room. You are a nice man Nico, but I don't think a romantic liaison between us would be wise. It would break my heart to lose you when you go home. I cannot do this."

She made to step past him and walk toward the door. Nico took hold of her arm and swung her back to him. He pulled her into his arms.

"Oh Isabelle. I am not asking for a convenient affair. Ti amo," he said.

She met his gaze, unsure of his words.

He smiled. "It means I love you. I love you Bella, and I want you," he said.

"Nico."

His lips descended and softly touched hers. His tongue swept into her mouth and a long sensual dance began between their tongues and mouths. Her fingers gripped tight to his jacket lapel, desperate to hold him close forever. Tender kisses were soon followed by deep passionate ones. Nico demanded all she could give him, and Isabelle found herself succumbing to his will.

She was his willing captive in this sensual embrace. She luxuriated in the sensual touch of a man. For far too long she had yearned for a man to want her. To touch her. To hold her in his arms and tell her she was his love.

Their bodies moved close against one another. As the kiss deepened, she heard him groan. It was all the encouragement she needed. Her hand slipped from his jacket and she placed it on his hip. She pulled herself hard to him, sighing as she felt the firmness of his manhood against her stomach.

Nico was hard. She pulled back from the kiss.

A sultry smile crept to her lips. She had aroused the beast. Their gazes met and she saw the glaze of passion in his eyes. The moment of truth had arrived.

"Do you consent?" he said.

Isabelle nodded. His asking for her permission meant everything. She would offer up her body to him, but it would be of her own free will.

"Good."

Placing his arm around her waist Nico lifted Isabelle and carried her over to the bed. He laid her gently down, then climbed onto the bed and straddled her.

"Trust me," he murmured in her ear.

She had expected him to strip her naked, but when he began to lift her skirts, she sensed he had other ideas.

A warm hand slid up the inside of her leg, stopping when it reached the thatch of her womanly hair. She arched her back as Nico slipped his thumb inside her wet heat. Slow measured strokes followed.

"I want you hot and begging for me Isabelle. I am going to take you fully clothed for our first time. Then when you are rested, I am going to slowly strip you and make love to you again."

She heard his words, but she was powerless to reply. Her mind was lost in a haze of sexual pleasure. His thumb continued to stroke, now rubbing hard against the nib of her clitoris.

Isabelle whimpered, desperate for release.

Nico pulled away. He threw off his jacket and opened the placket of his trousers. Isabelle caught sight of the wonder of his engorged manhood. She licked her dry lips, hungry for his attention.

He lifted her skirts free from about her waist, then settled over her. He guided his hard member to her entrance, then slowly entered her.

Isabelle lay back and closed her eyes, rejoicing in the knowledge that he was now inside her. That Nico was going to make her his. When he thrust deep the first time she sobbed and clutched her hands to his hips.

"Open your eyes Bella. I want you to watch me make love to you," he said.

She did as he commanded. Her heart soaring with happiness as he rewarded her with a deep kiss.

Making love in a well-lit room was a new and heady experience for her. As Nico rocked his hips back and forth, thrusting in and out, she watched the passion of their love making play out on his face. It was the most beautiful thing she had ever seen.

He settled over her and began to grind against her sensitive nib.

"Take me deep. Let me bring you to completion," he said.

She opened her legs wider, sobbing with desperate need as he plundered her willing body. On and on he pushed her higher. At the summit, she teetered on the edge before he finally pushed her over into an orgasm that had her crying his name.

His own release soon followed. "Bella. I will never stop wanting you," he said.

Chapter Sixteen

"You are a very generous lover. I expect you have heard that before, but still I wanted to say it," said Isabelle.

Nico pulled her close to him, kissing her on the forehead as she wrapped her arms around him and lay her head on his chest. His heart was pounding loudly in his chest from the exertion of having ridden her hard and long. His climax still coursed through his body in waves of pleasure.

He had been unsure of what would happen once they returned to London, fearing that Isabelle's concerns about Ann's good opinion would keep her from his bed.

His worries had been swept away when Isabelle came to his room the night they returned from Surrey. After stripping naked for him, she had climbed into his bed and made love to him.

Their sexual encounters now increased in fervor the longer they spent together. There was a growing boldness in the way she came to him. The shy and hesitant young widow had now transformed into a sexually aggressive minx who was hungry and demanding of his body. Isabelle was beyond anything Nico had ever hoped for in a lover.

"I could say the same of you. You hold nothing of yourself back when we are together. It should always be that way between us, even after we marry," he replied.

He brushed his fingers lightly over her breast. When the nipple immediately hardened, he wondered how long it would be until she was aroused a second time. He intended to take her at least once more before they slept. And before she slipped back to her room in the early pre-dawn, he would make it a third.

She sat up and turned to him. When their gazes met, Nico sensed a change in the mood.

"Are we to marry? I can understand if you see this as a passionate, but short-lived affair," she replied.

He shuffled over in the bed and sat up next to her. Placing a hand under her chin he leaned in and placed a soft kiss on her lips.

"We will marry," he said.

The words were said, but they lacked the certainty that he had assumed they would. Isabelle nodded slowly.

"I expect that is where things will eventually land, but I am not certain of the path we will take," she replied.

To his disappointment, she climbed off the bed and picked up her nightgown. Nico clambered off the bed and took a hold of her gown. They wrestled with it for a moment before he reluctantly let go.

"Why won't you stay the night in my bed? This is your house. There is no need for you to be creeping about the hallways," he said.

Isabelle slipped her nightgown over her head.

"You are wrong on both counts. This is your house; and we have a house full of servants, not to mention a mother in law to avoid. If word got out that I am having a liaison with an Italian count, there would be the devil to pay."

Nico huffed. He was both annoyed and insulted at her words.

"But what about when they find out that you and I are to marry? None of this will matter to them, so why should it matter to us?"

She stopped lacing up the front of her gown and took hold of his hand.

"You appear to have this all figured out Nico. But from where I stand things are not so clear. Where for instance are we to live, have you even considered that not so insignificant matter?" she replied.

He looked down at her hand and frowned. He had assumed the situation would be the same as for his parents. Isabelle, like his mother, would happily go to live in Rome, returning home to England every few years or so.

"I love you Nico, but I loved Anthony as well. I gave up everything for him and look where it got me. A widow and penniless. A tenant in my own home as the result of a husband who sold the very ground out from under me. I cannot just throw my whole life in with you, without you giving something back. I won't be a man's puppet again, not for anyone," she said.

She released his hand and stepped back. There were tears shining in her eyes when he looked up. He sucked in a deep breath.

"I cannot live in England. You know how much pain this country has brought to my life. I might be half English, but my blood is that of an Italian. I need to feel the heat of the Mediterranean sun on my face. I have to walk the cobbled streets of Rome in order to feed my soul. The foul air of London suffocates me," he replied.

"And yet it is my home."

Isabelle finished lacing up her nightgown and slipped her arms into her dressing gown. She reached up and placed a tender, soft kiss on Nico's lips.

"Now you can understand why we need to keep this relationship a secret. Neither of us wants to be put in a position where we have to marry."

He let her leave without trying to stop her.

"Bloody hell," he muttered.

He snorted, angry with himself for not even being able to curse in his native tongue. Two weeks in England and already the place was getting under his skin.

Isabelle was like Elizabeth in one respect, she was looking at this logically. While he like his father was thinking with his heart. He loved her, she loved him. Everything else would be sorted out over time. Emotions were what mattered, not cold-hearted planning. The English had the whole business of marriage the wrong way around.

Passion was the fuel of the world, not the wording of a marriage settlement.

"Stubborn woman," he muttered.

Isabelle closed her bedroom door. The only consolation of tonight's disagreement was that she had finally put voice to her growing misgivings. Nico now understood her mind and her concerns.

"Foolish man," she muttered.

Foolish me.

While thoughts of being with Nico and sailing off to a new life with him had been merely dreams she had not had to think too hard about the realities she would have to face. Now as her future seemed secure doubt had crept into her mind.

For the second time in her life she was being asked to give up her home in order to secure love. Marrying Anthony and then losing him had left her virtually alone in the world. If she married Nico and their love failed, she would have nowhere to go.

Her current life, however tenuous was familiar. She could find a suitable husband and remain in England. Nico expected her to throw her whole lot in with him, yet he risked nothing more than a broken heart.

From where she stood, it was a choice between security or love.

"And this is why we need to keep our relationship a secret you stubborn man," she said.

If it came to it she could go back onto the marriage market and no one would ever know about her affair with Count Nico de Luca.

She placed a hand softly on her stomach.

What if it is already too late.

She had lain with him enough times over the past week for the possibility of a child to already be growing within her. A child she would have to sacrifice everything for if it came to it.

Isabelle threw off her dressing gown and climbed into her cold bed. Nico would have to yield something in order to secure her promise to marry him. She would never again sign over complete control of her life and future into the hands of a man.

Chapter Seventeen

Nico rolled over and faced the wall. For hours he had been tossing and turning. Something wasn't right. The argument with Isabelle was clear enough in his mind, and he would deal with it in good time. He was Italian, he was used to dealing with strong women.

It was what she had said about the house that had him staring up at the shadows of the flames from the fireplace as they danced on the ceiling.

A husband who sold the very ground out from under me.

Isabelle was convinced Anthony had sold the house before his untimely death.

Throwing off the bed clothes Nico hurried over to the wardrobe and opened it. In quick time he had dressed and grabbed his thick, warm overcoat. It was two o'clock in the morning, but since he stood little chance of getting any sleep, the least he could do with his time was to make good use of it.

There was only one way to get to the truth of his ownership of the house. All the accounts for his business holdings in England were kept at the shipping office in Wapping. Once he had sorted through the books of account he would have a clearer picture.

If he could prove that Anthony had not sold the house while he still lived, Isabelle might be more amenable to discussing her future. With that piece of truth in her possession he hoped she would finally come to terms with her husband's death and be able to move forward with her life.

Nico slipped out the front door of the house and hailed a hack. With few carriages on the street at that time of night, he was able to make the five-mile journey to Wapping Street in good time.

Once outside, he headed up to the front door. The night watchman was fast asleep in his office. The thought of waking the man and reprimanding him crossed Nico's mind, but he wasn't in the mood for more confrontation this night.

Taking his key out of his coat pocket his quietly opened the door, locking it behind him as he stepped across the threshold. A second key on the keyring opened Prescott's office upstairs.

Once inside he lit a lamp and set it down on Prescott's desk. He surveyed the office. The most recent books of account would be in Prescott's desk, ready for easy access. The purchase of the house at New Cavendish Street had occurred two years prior, so the books of account for that time were likely to be in the archives.

"So where would you keep the older files?" he muttered.

He began to open the nearby cupboards, all of which were full of neatly stacked shipping records. His heart sank. It would take him hours to find the right book of account at this rate.

"Stupido," he cursed himself.

He didn't need the books of account, he needed the title deed for the house. In the bottom drawer of Prescott's desk, he located a wooden box. Inside the box was a stack of neatly folded papers. All of them title deeds to the properties the de Luca family owned in London.

"Successo! he exclaimed.

Taking a seat at Prescott's desk, he sorted through the title deeds until he found the one marked *Certificate of Title for House and Freehold Land at New Cavendish Street, City of Westminster, London.*

He opened the folio and ran his finger down the list of owners. The third last owner had been Anthony's father. Then came Anthony. Then the Duchy of Lazio, Rome.

The list should have been simple enough but something in the margin after Anthony's name caught his eye.

In settlement of all debts I transfer ownership to P Prescott. By my signature Anthony Collins. August 1813. Brighton.

Nico sat back in the chair and stared at the title deed. What the devil did those words mean?

"Your Excellency?"

Nico looked up with a start at the night watchman who was standing in the doorway. He had been so lost in the words on the title deed, he had not heard the man open the door.

"Ah. Good evening. I was in the area and thought I could get a head start on working through the books of account. You must have been doing your rounds when I arrived," said Nico.

The night watchman quickly nodded his head.

"Yes. I was checking the locks and doors in the rear laneway. There are some ruffians about, so I don't take any chances when it comes to making sure everything is safe and secure here, your lordship," he replied.

An uneasy silence followed before Nico realized that the man was waiting for him to dismiss him from his presence.

"Well then. I shall let you get back to your business. I won't be here long. I shall tidy up these papers and then head home for a night cap. Good night," he said.

The night watchman bowed and beat a hasty retreat. Nico watched him go, in the full knowledge that the night watchman would be making a great show of checking every lock and window while his master was still on the premises. He doubted the man would be making mention to anyone of Nico's unannounced visit this evening, considering the questions it might raise about his own sleeping habits.

After the night watchman had gone, Nico sat and stared at the title deed again. A hundred thoughts rolled around in his head. All of which came back to the one that made his skin crawl.

Phillip Prescott had known Anthony Collins before he died. The purchase of the house had not been through some arms-length business transaction, it had been in settlement of a debt.

He glanced a look at the cupboard full of books of account. Getting home and sleeping were no longer of his concern. He needed answers before he left the office, even if it took him all night to find them.

From out of his coat pocket he produced his hip flask and set it down on the desk. It was going to be a long night and he would need the warmth from the brandy.

Back at the cupboard he opened the door and stood staring at the piles of account books. He picked up one, then looked at the next book under it. They were in dated sequential order. Prescott was nothing if not neat and orderly in his book work and filing.

By following the order of the piles of books, he came across the set dated 1813, the year that Anthony Collins had died.

He resumed his seat at the desk and began to work through the pages. Two hours later, he pushed back from the desk and got to his feet. It had taken a good deal of checking and rechecking to finally put the trail of numbers together.

He had to hand it to Phillip Prescott, he had been thorough in his efforts to cover his tracks. But the numbers did not lie. Somewhere in the latter part of 1810 he had begun to embezzle funds from the de Luca family company. While the entries looked to be legitimate, the items in various columns of the books did not actually add to the total written at the bottom.

It was only when the purchase of the Collins house in 1813 was included in the accounts that they finally tallied up once more.

He clenched his fists. The rage that coursed through his body took away all worries of the chill night air.

According to Isabelle, Anthony Collins had been a gambler, reckless to the end. Had his final shameful act been to lose his house in a game of chance to Phillip Prescott?

Prescott who in turn had then covered up his own fraud by pretending he had bought the house on behalf of Nico's company. A house that was worth far more than the money Prescott had registered as its purchase price.

A wave of nausea washed over Nico. He had benefitted from Anthony's gambling losses and Isabelle had been left to pay the price.

He packed up the books of account for the years between 1810 and 1813 and put them neatly back in the cupboard. He kept the title deed for New Cavendish Street. Then locking up Prescott's desk and office he headed back downstairs.

Once outside in the street, he looked back up at the office. In the morning Prescott would arrive at work and go about his business, oblivious to the fact that Nico had uncovered his dirty, fraudulent scheme.

"I will bring you down you bastard," he muttered.

From his coat pocket he retrieved the business card his uncle had given him. He walked to the end of Shakespeare's Walk and hailed a hack.

It was close on six o'clock by the time the carriage reached its destination on the other side of London. The sun was yet to rise.

"Wait here," he instructed the driver.

He walked up to the front door of the large manor house and rapped loudly on it. Some minutes later a small hunched man opened the front door. He held a cocked pistol in his hand.

Nico looked down at him and nodded.

"Tell your master Count Nico de Luca wishes to speak with him. I have an urgent matter of business which needs his attention."

He followed the butler inside and closed the door behind him.

Chapter Eighteen

Isabelle deliberately slept late the following morning in the hope that she would avoid having to speak to Nico. When she finally did come down for breakfast at nearly eleven o'clock she found Ann waiting for her in the breakfast room.

"I was wondering when you were going to make an appearance," said Ann.

Isabelle took a seat at the table and waited while a servant poured her a cup of coffee and brought her some fresh toast from the downstairs kitchen.

"I was tired last night and must have overslept,' she replied.

Ann snorted. "If you are looking to avoid our guest, I wouldn't worry about it. From what the servants tell me he left the house sometime just after midnight and has not returned. I expect he decided to find himself a nice spot in a gentleman's club and work his way through several large glasses of brandy."

"What do you mean avoid him?" replied Isabelle.

Ann rose from her chair and quickly dismissed the maid and footman who were standing to one side of the table. Isabelle was certain she heard the maid huff as she left the room.

Ann locked the door and then came to sit by Isabelle's side.

"It's easy to forget that one of the pitfalls of having servants is that they all have ears for listening in to private conversations," she said.

Isabelle managed a wane smile for Ann's benefit.

"I am not avoiding Nico. I just don't think we need to be in each other's company continually while he is here. People might start to get ideas," she replied.

Ann's huff in reply matched that of the disappointed maid.

"Pish posh. I am not blind to what has been going on. The floor boards in this house have always had a peculiar squeak about them. It's how I always knew when Anthony was trying to steal quietly into the house after a night at the gaming tables. It is obvious that there has been movement between your room and Nico's in the early hours of the morning. Well at least since you came back from Surrey. Don't tell me you two have had a lover's tiff."

Isabelle picked up her coffee and took a sip. Of course, Ann had figured things out, she had been a fool to think otherwise.

"He wants us to marry and for me to go back to Italy with him. He hates England and says he could never live here. I told him I don't think I can give up my home for him," replied Isabelle.

Ann reached out and took hold of Isabelle's hand.

"And why not? From the look on your face I would say you were hopelessly in love with him. If I had thought for one minute that his attentions were not welcomed by you I would have thrown him and his fine travel trunk out into the street long ago."

Memories of Nico's hands and lips on her naked body filled Isabelle's mind. His attentions had been more than welcome. They had been a god send in her cold empty widow's existence. The thought of throwing away the opportunity to be his wife filled her with dismay. Was she being an irrational fool?

"He would never do that. Nico is a gentleman to his bones. The relationship has been by mutual consent. And to tell the truth I love him. I just don't know if I can put my life and future into the hands of a man again. I barely knew much about Anthony before we married, and I know even less of Nico. To throw it all in and get on a boat with him to a strange country is an enormous leap of faith. There is also the matter of your good self," said Isabelle.

"Ah. I was wondering when we would get to that part. Well let me set you straight. I have plans to go and live with my cousin in Somerset as soon as I am rid of you. Why do you think I am in such a hurry to get you a new husband?" replied Ann.

Isabelle chanced a look at Ann. Her brave words were in stark contrast to the tears that shone in Ann's eyes. She leaned over and placed a kiss on Ann's cheek.

"Wouldn't you at least want me to marry an Englishman, someone who will keep me here in England?"

Ann shook her head.

"No. Because I will be damned if I will let you marry purely for money. You have a beautiful heart Isabelle and a man such as Nico deserves to hold it. If you love him, then tell him so, and make him agree to a life you can live by. Make him give up something that he values for you."

Isabelle looked to where Nico normally sat for breakfast and sighed. Ann had such a way of seeing things clearly, while she was left wasting hours as the same words rolled around in her mind until her head ached.

Rather than making demands of him, she should be negotiating like any good wife would do. He had made his opening offer, and she had foolishly taken it as his first and final. It was time for her to get back to the negotiating table.

"Thank you. You have always had the best advice when it came to men," Isabelle replied.

"I wish that was the case. I failed terribly when it came to my son. Instead of encouraging the match, I should have told you to run for the hills," replied Ann.

Isabelle drained the last of the coffee from her cup. They had all made mistakes when it came to Anthony, but now she had the chance to make a fresh start. It was up to her to decide the sort of future she wanted with Nico. After that there only remained the small problem of getting him to agree to her plans.

"I shall wait for him to return to the house this morning, and when he is in an agreeable mood I shall talk to him."

They finished breakfast and Isabelle was headed back upstairs when the butler caught up with her.

"His lordship came back while you were having breakfast. He packed a travel bag and left a few minutes ago. He asked that I give you this." He handed Isabelle a folded and sealed letter.

She turned it over, frowning when she saw Nico's personal seal on the back. A chill of dread filled her. The last thing she wanted was for him to have taken last night's disagreement as being her final word. God forbid he had taken himself off to a hotel for the rest of his stay.

"Did he say when he was coming back?" she asked.

The butler shook his head.

In the privacy of her room Isabelle opened the letter. She drew in a deep breath to calm her shaking hands as she pulled it open.

> *Dearest Isabelle,*
> *An urgent matter has come up and I have had to leave*
>   *London. My apologies for the short notice.*
> *Nico.*

She turned the page over. The brief note was all he had written. "What have I done?" she cried.

Chapter Nineteen

Nico stepped down from the travel coach and smiled as he caught sight of the blue sea of the English Channel. The sea was in his blood.

"It's a bit brisk out this morning, I hope you don't find it too cold."

He wiped the sleep from his eyes and turned to his travelling companion. The private investigator his uncle's man of business had hired for him looked a little worse for wear from the overnight coach trip down from London.

"Actually, I love the sea breeze at Brighton. I used to come here quite often when I was a school boy in England. The smell of the sea always reminded me of home," he replied.

Nico stretched his arms and worked out some of the kinks in his muscles. After having not seen his bed for two days, he had done his best to get sleep on the journey to the popular seaside town. His travelling companion, Mr. Donovan had not been so fortunate.

Several times Nico had woken during the night to see Donovan staring out the carriage window, a pained look on his face.

"How is your back this morning Mr. Donovan? If I had known it would make the journey so uncomfortable for you, I would not have asked you to come," he said.

Donovan waved his concerns away.

"Thank you, my lord. I shall have a few glasses of brandy after we have concluded our morning business, then lie down on the floor of my hotel room for an hour or so. Once the muscles have had an opportunity to relax I shall be fine."

Nico picked up his travel bag and started for the front steps of the Old Ship hotel. The sooner they were checked in, the sooner he could get to the answers he needed.

"You did say the first place for us to go was Shoals on Lewes Crescent. How long will it take us to reach there? I am keen to get things underway and be back in London as soon as possible," said Nico.

He had left a brief note for Isabelle telling her he had to leave London to attend to a personal matter but was now beginning to regret having left the house in such haste.

You always rush into things without thinking them through. She probably read your note and thinks you have abandoned her.

He frowned at the thought, angry with himself for being too eager to get to the truth of Phillip Prescott and Anthony Collins.

"It is a mile or so from here. I was going to send word ahead but thought perhaps it would be better if I didn't. I understand from my brief investigations in London, that the Shoals club does not open until later in the morning. If this is a sensitive matter we would not want to give advance notice of our arrival," replied Donovan.

Nico stirred from his private musings.

"Yes. We shall go later in the day. And since we do not know who else was involved in the events of the day that Anthony Collins disappeared a quiet approach would be best," he replied.

Donovan cleared his throat and nodded toward the front door. Nico could tell he was eager to get inside and find respite from his bad back.

"Go ahead, I might take the opportunity to have a walk around the town and reacquaint myself," said Nico.

He handed his travel bag to a footman and walked away from the hotel, along the street which fronted the beach. Groups of well-dressed people passed him by, reminding him that Brighton was the favourite seaside home for the rich and powerful of London. Wherever the Prince Regent played, the fast crowd of the *ton* were sure to follow.

After crossing several streets, he turned left and headed up East Street toward the Royal Pavilion. Long before he reached the end of the street he caught sight of a large half-built dome, surrounded by scaffolding and teams of workmen.

He stopped and took in the view. What he had remembered as a simple, but elegant building was being transformed into a garish faux eastern themed monstrosity. On either side of the giant onion shaped dome were set what appeared to be a poor attempt at matching minarets.

He shook his head in disgust. He had seen the grand Hagia Sophia in Istanbul on which the design was clearly based. And in Nico's opinion the new architect of the Royal Pavilion was destined to build a disaster rather than a loving homage to the great mosque.

"Each to his own," he muttered.

A horse and cart carrying a large stone block forced him to one side of the road. It was followed by another.

He took his cue and turned back the way he had come. Casual visitors would not be welcome around the building site.

Reaching the hotel, he was greeted by Donovan.

"Good news. I managed to speak to one of the staff here and they know the owner of the Shoals. He has agreed to meet with us this morning," he said.

"Good. Let me freshen up in my room and I shall join you within the hour," replied Nico.

&

A little after midday Nico and Donovan stood in the small receiving parlor at Shoals club. A butler brought them both a glass of whisky. Donovan downed his in one gulp, while Nico set his down on a nearby table untouched.

He wanted his mind to be perfectly clear. If his hunch was proven right, he needed to be able to give Isabelle an exact retelling of the discussion surrounding her husband's disappearance and subsequent death.

"Good morning."

A well-dressed but very overweight man stood in the doorway. "Good morning, my name is Count Nico de Luca," replied Nico.

The sound of Nico's grand name had an immediate effect. The man dipped into a half bow, which was the best his large girth could permit. He made up for his lack of dexterity by adding a graceful sweep of his hand.

Donovan gave Nico a telling look. One which said he had already stamped the gentleman as someone not to be trusted.

"Albert Williams, I am the manager of this fine establishment and have been for the past twenty years. Were you two gentlemen looking to play at the tables today, if you are then may I suggest you have a few of our complimentary drinks while you wait for more patrons to arrive?"

Donovan stepped forward, but Nico placed a hand on his shoulder.

"Sir, I have travelled from Rome. For my mother. Her nephew Anthony died here two years past. She is how you say, sad and needs to know what happened," said Nico.

He caught the frown on Donovan's face at Nico's broken English. But Nico had learned his lessons well from his time in England as a boy. People who thought him incapable of speaking the King's English tended to trip themselves up. While he mangled the local language, they in turn often gave up more information than they would have if he had asked in his usual fluent way.

A telling bright red patch appeared on the manager's face.

"Oh."

He looked from Nico to Donovan, but neither changed their expression. With a shrug he offered them both a seat.

"I will tell you what I told the local authorities after the unfortunate incident. Your cousin, Mr. Collins and another regular customer started to play cards. The first game would have been around five o'clock and they continued playing non-stop. The other gentleman, a Mr. Prescott appeared to be on a sudden winning streak and by the time I passed the table at about ten o'clock he had a substantial pile of coins and notes in front of him. Mr. Collins was becoming quite distressed."

Sweat began to pour down the side of William's neck and he fidgeted in his pocket for a handkerchief. He dabbed at his face and neck as Nico and Donovan both sat silently waiting.

"Well. A little later one of my staff came to tell me that he had seen a pistol being drawn and placed on the table. This is a respectable establishment and of course I went to speak to the two gentlemen," he continued.

Donovan cleared his throat.

"So, when you spoke to the two gentlemen, who actually had the pistol in front of him?" he asked.

Nico ground his teeth silently, trying to imagine how the heightened tension between the two gamblers would have reached boiling point at the sight of a gun.

"Mr. Collins had the gun. He was most agitated when I asked him to put it away. Mr. Prescott on the other hand did not appear to find offense at having a loaded pistol on the table. He was calm. Very calm."

Nico sat forward in his chair and clasped his hands together.

"Did my cousin call for a pen and ink?" he asked.

The color drained from Albert William's face and his hands began to shake. When he nodded, Nico sensed he was close to tears.

"I tried to stop him. He pulled a title deed from out of his pocket and slapped it down on the table. He put the pistol on top and said something to the effect that either he won it all back that night or he would kill himself. A half hour later, he asked for pen and ink so he could sign over the title deed to Mr. Prescott. After that he went outside and from what the authorities later told me he shot himself."

An eerie silence descended on the room. Williams sat clutching his sweat soaked handkerchief tightly in his hands. Donovan got up and walked over to the window and looked outside.

Nico toyed with his signet ring. Anthony Collins had lost his house in a game of cards and in the shameful aftermath had killed himself. Phillip Prescott in turn had taken the title deed to what should have been Isabelle's home and used it to cover up a long-standing fraud against the de Luca family. Nico gritted his teeth so hard that his jaw protested.

"Tell me something Mr. Williams. Did Prescott know Mr. Collins before that night?" asked Donovan.

Nico's head shot up.

"Yes. They had played one another many times over the years. Mr. Prescott actually helped with the delicate matter of removing Mr. Collins' body back to London. I thought that was particularly gallant of him," replied Williams.

Nico got to his feet. He had heard enough. Phillip Prescott clearly knew how to play Anthony Collins and when the golden opportunity to cover up all his previous financial misdeeds presented itself, he had not hesitated to press home his advantage.

He had then comforted Isabelle while she waited on news of her husband, all the while knowing Anthony was already dead. The paperwork to put the house into Nico's name was a simple enough task. With that done, he had washed his hands of the whole sordid mess.

"Thank you for your time. I think I have heard all I need. My mother will understand," he said.

Standing on the front steps of the gambling house a few minutes later, Nico looked down at the finely polished black and white geometric tiles. Isabelle's dreams, along with Anthony had died on this very spot. Phillip Prescott may have won the final game of cards, but it had been Nico de Luca who had directly benefitted from Isabelle's heavy loss.

A sickening feeling settled in the pit of his stomach. Isabelle had to be told the truth. How she would take hearing the truth of Anthony's death and the loss of her home was a challenge he would have to face.

With a heavy heart he followed Donovan down the steps and into the street. With love finally within his grasp he feared to lose it. Isabelle was the one thing he had yearned for his entire adult life. A woman who loved him for himself and who would stand beside him for the rest of his days.

Climbing back into the coach, he ignored Donovan's suggestion about making plans for dinner. He couldn't stomach the thought of food.

Chapter Twenty

"He has returned," said Ann. Isabelle didn't need to ask to whom Ann was referring. For the past three days she had thought of little else but the look of hurt on Nico's face when she told him of her reservations about them marrying. She steeled herself for seeing him once more.

"Do you think I should go and talk to him?" she replied.

Ann shook her head. "No, let him get settled back into his room. When he is ready he will seek you out."

The same sickening sense of foreboding Isabelle had known when the executor for Anthony's estate had arrived two years earlier now gripped her mind. Was she once more destined to have her life ripped out from under her. Did Nico still want her? He had left in a hurry, and his note had been perfunctory to say the least.

The door of the sitting room opened.

Isabelle held her hands clasped in her lap but did not look in the direction of the door. The rustle of Ann's skirts as she left the room was enough to tell her who was standing in the doorway.

At the sound of the door clicking shut, she held her breath.

"Bella?"

The pleading in his voice was heart breaking. She looked up to see Nico holding his hand out to her. The air rushed out of her lungs as she took his hand and he pulled her to her feet.

Strong arms wrapped around her body, taking her in his loving embrace. For a long moment, they stood in silence simply holding one another.

When Nico finally released Isabelle, he cupped her face in his hands and drew her to him. Warm lips touched. She closed her eyes and gave into the sweet seduction of his kiss. As their tongues met, she sensed the hunger within him. A hunger she shared.

The days since she had last seen him had been an eternity of torture. Wondering when he would walk back through the door, hoping against all hope that she had not pushed him away.

Nico.

"I have missed you,' he murmured when they finally broke the kiss.

She looked up at him, capturing his gaze. Those deep brown eyes held all the forgiveness she ached for from him.

"We need to talk," they said in unison.

He brushed his fingers through her soft fringe, then leaned in once more to kiss her. "Bella."

A shy moment passed between them, even Nico seemed unsure of himself.

"I'm sorry for being so stubborn about our future, I hope you can understand," she said.

He sighed. "We can talk about that later, but first there is something else we need to discuss. Something which has to be dealt with before we can settle on our marriage," he said.

Isabelle tried to remain calm. Whatever they had to deal with was of major importance.

They took a seat on the low couch side by side. Nico placed Isabelle's hand in his.

"I have been to Brighton in search of answers about Anthony," he said.

She frowned. Anthony had died in Brighton, but what did that have to do with Nico?

"Phillip Prescott, is not what he would appear to be, he is a gambler who embezzled a large amount of money from me over the years. He was only able to cover up the fraud by the fact that he won a house in a game of cards. This house."

"But Anthony sold the house. He...oh no," she replied. Her hand went to her mouth.

"My investigations have uncovered the fact that Anthony was already dead when Prescott sat and waited with you for news of your missing husband."

Isabelle swayed as shock reverberated throughout her body. Her mind went blank as she struggled to process Nico's words. She pushed Nico's hand away and got to her feet, burning anger sparked in her mind. Pacing back and forth, she fought to keep her wrath in check.

"How did you find out?" she eventually asked.

The past could not be changed, but she had to know the whole truth. Nico started to his feet, but Isabelle motioned for him to remain seated. She needed distance between them in order to think. Being close to him would only cloud her mind.

"I had my doubts about several things not long after I arrived. Offering for me to stay here when you clearly couldn't afford to run the house made little sense. When you told me that Prescott had made a deal to let you stay rent free for six months I must confess the hairs on the back of neck stood on end. I determined at that moment to discover the truth," he replied.

Nico got to his feet but kept his distance. From out of his coat pocket he took a folded leather satchel and set it down on a nearby table.

"I went to the shipping office the night you and I had our argument. You said Anthony sold the house, yet Prescott had always maintained he purchased it from a deceased estate. It may have been a simple misuse of words on his part, but since I couldn't sleep

I decided to get to the bottom of matters. That is when I discovered the title deed to the house. Anthony had signed it over to Prescott before his death."

She held his gaze, nodding as realization finally took hold. Anthony had gambled the house away and Prescott had used it as a means to cover up his crime. "But what difference does that make to you and me?" she replied.

While she was grateful for Nico's efforts it was cold comfort to know the truth over two years after the event.

"It makes a difference because I have benefited from your misfortune. My theory is that Prescott decided to give you free rent in order to provide you with the opportunity to marry your way out of poverty and back into society. With you and Ann gone from this house he could then close out one of the last chances of me ever discovering the truth. Of course, he didn't count on you and I falling for one another."

"I suppose none of us did," she replied.

Isabelle clenched her fists. At this moment, she was unsure as to whom she hated more. Anthony or Prescott. Both had been instrumental in the misery which had been her lot as a widow. Both had much for which to answer.

But only one of them was alive. She could have her justice if she chose to move against Prescott. Nico would be in possession of enough evidence to see Prescott put to trial. She owed it both to herself and Ann to seek justice.

"Does Prescott know that you have discovered his secret?" she asked.

"No," replied Nico. He ventured over to Isabelle and despite her protests pulled her into his arms. She closed her eyes. There was an overwhelming sense of security in being with him. An iron clad confirmation that he would never betray her. Nico de Luca would stand fast to his last breath and protect her from the world.

When he finally released her from his embrace, he picked up the satchel from the table and handed it to Isabelle.

"Open it please," he said.

She reluctantly opened it. There were two documents inside. The first was the deed to the house. As she read Anthony's scrawled note of transfer she fought back tears. The very last words he had written in his life stared coldly back at her.

When she opened the second document she immediately lost the battle against her tears. "What is this for?" she sobbed, holding it toward Nico with a shaking hand.

He pointed to the papers.

"I am giving you the house. The bank promissory letter represents the difference in the price which you should have received on a fair market sale of the house. I have also added in back payment of the rent you have paid since I took ownership. Together they will ensure that you have choices with regard to your future. As you are at this moment a widow, you can own the property in your own name. If you choose to remain a widow no man, including me, will ever again hold your future in his hands," he said.

"I don't want this, I want you," she replied, shoving the papers roughly back into his hands. A look of relief appeared on his face.

"I was hoping you would say that Isabelle. Rest assured however, I will settle money on you before our marriage. Funds that no one will ever be able to touch without your agreement. If anything, ever happens, you will have all that you need," he said.

Her silent plea for him to touch her once again was granted. Nico offered his lips to her in a tender kiss to which she responded by seizing the lapel of his coat and pulling him hard to him. She didn't want to think about Prescott, or money or even the house.

She needed Nico.

It had been too many days since they had lain together and her gnawing hunger for him burned deep. She lifted the tempo of their engagement, offering her mouth fully to him.

When Isabelle began to back toward the couch, intent on offering her body for his pleasure, he pulled back. She mewled with disappointment.

"Not yet, not until the matter of what we are going to do about Prescott is settled. Believe me Isabelle I want nothing more than to be inside you right this minute, but I want to be fully in the moment when I take you. Nothing on my mind but the thought of giving you pleasure and hearing you cry out at your completion," he ground out.

Her disappointment at his reluctance to strip her naked and take her was tempered by the knowledge that he desired her as much as she wanted him. But for now, their moment of passion and intimacy would have to wait.

The matter of Prescott and what to do about him had to be addressed. She withdrew from Nico's embrace and looked at the documents on the table. Forgery and embezzlement were serious crimes, ones which carried the death penalty if successfully proven in court.

"You no doubt have had time to think about Prescott on the road back to London. I am surprised that you have not already had him arrested," she said.

"I plan to move against him, but since the crime is truly against you I need to hear you say the words. I will seek justice for you, but only at your command," he replied.

This was an unexpected development. For the first time in her life a man was handing Isabelle real power. A man was asking for her opinion on matters of importance in her life. The one man who she knew would listen.

"You know that I love you," she said.

"Yes, and I love you too. Which is why I want us to be in complete agreement as to what is to be done. If we are to embark on a life together, we need to act as one," he replied.

Unlike so many of the conversations she had had with Anthony, Isabelle knew Nico would be true to his word. Nico was different. He valued her opinion, a gift which was as precious as his love. But she was unsure of how to deal with this unexpected power.

"I need time to think this through. If Prescott believes he got away with this fraud a long time ago, then he is not likely to make any sudden moves. A day or so delay on our part should not make a difference," she said.

Nico nodded.

"Agreed, but I need your answer sooner rather than later. We cannot run the risk that Prescott does decide to check the box of titles and discovers one of them missing. It would put him to flight," he replied.

Chapter Twenty-One

I sabelle stuffed her feet into her soft leather boots. With her long woolen coat, and a scarf wrapped around her neck and over the back of her head she was rugged up well against the bitter winter wind.

Stepping out the front door of the house, she stood on the side of the street and put on her gloves. After the shock of Nico's revelations, she needed time alone to think.

The one way she was sure to have a clear mind was by walking. In the months following Anthony's untimely death she had tallied up many foot sore miles in order to keep her sanity.

Turning left out of New Cavendish Street, she headed away from the shops and crowded streets of central London. Nearby Green Lane was her destination.

Fields of cows and vegetable gardens stretched out before her. In the fields the local gardeners were busy picking vegetables for sale in the city markets. A farmer was herding his milking cows toward a shed for their evening milking. The ebb and flow of life continued as it had for many centuries in the lands around the city of London.

Isabelle pressed on, seeking out her favorite thinking spot.

Under a horse chestnut tree, she finally stopped. An enterprising craftsman had built a wooden bench which encircled the bottom of the tree. Oftentimes when she had visited this spot families were seated on the bench taking a rest on the long walk back from the markets to the local villages.

Isabelle was pleased to find that at this time there was no one else under the tree. She needed solace in order to think. She took a seat on the far side of the tree out of the wind.

"Oh Anthony. You, poor man," she whispered.

While Nico had been concerned about her welfare and what was to be done about Phillip Prescott, she had the added pain of absorbing the truth about her husband's death. What had been explained to her and Ann as an unfortunate accident had been something far more tragic.

Faced with the loss of his home and knowing the pain it would cause his family, Anthony Collins had taken his own life. While love had long ago died between them, she still felt pity for a man who had been consumed by his addiction.

She clenched her fists as tight as her gloves would allow. In his distressed state Anthony had chosen death as the honorable way out.

"If only I had been there Anthony. I could have told you that there is no honor in death," she whispered.

She slowly let her hands relax and wiped away bitter tears.

"Come on Isabelle, do not think of impossible what-ifs. Focus on what needs to be done. The past is the past."

Nico had given her time to decide on what they were to do about Prescott. She owed it to him and to their future to frame a sensible decision.

A group of women farm laborers who were passing by gave Isabelle a friendly wave. She had spent so many days walking the roads and laneways of the area that some of the locals now considered her to be one of them. She waved back. It was nice to feel welcome, to have a sense of belonging.

As they approached, Isabelle rose to greet them. After the battle of Waterloo there were many widows and orphans of English soldiers left to eke out a new life working the market gardens.

"Hello Mrs. Collins nice to see you on this fine day. We haven't seen you in a bit," said one of the women

"Hello Polly," she replied.

Isabelle reached down and ruffled the hair of a small lad who appeared from behind Polly's skirts. "Isabelle! You came," the boy exclaimed.

She looked down at his expectant face and her heart dropped.

"Oh. I forgot. I am so sorry Nathaniel. I left the book on the stand right next to the front door. I was in such a hurry to leave the house I completely forgot," she said.

His shoulders dropped as disappointment registered on his face.

"Now don't you mind Mrs. Collins, it was very kind of you to offer to lend Nathaniel one of your books. I am sure there will be another time," said Polly.

Isabelle bent down and put her arms around Nathaniel's waist, lifting him up as she stood.

"A promise is a promise. I said I would bring the book and I shall do just that for you. I will return tomorrow at this time and bring the book with me. Gulliver's Travels you were promised and Gulliver's Travels you shall have," she said.

Nathaniel gave her a cheeky kiss. He dropped to the ground and ran off in the direction of the milking barn.

"How have you been Polly?" asked Isabelle once they were alone.

Polly screwed up her nose. "Prices at the market are getting better with more food shortages, but it just means that we can only eat simple food in order to make rent ourselves. My sister has written to me from Bedford and offered for us to come up and live with her, but I don't know if it is going to be any better there. I've heard further north that people are beginning to starve," she replied.

Isabelle nodded. It was odd to think that a volcanic eruption in a far-off land could impact the weather so badly across England and Europe. The oddly colored skies that they had seen since earlier that year had been the first sign that something was very wrong in the world.

"Yes, well let me know if you need any assistance. I will do all I can,' replied Isabelle.

Polly smiled. "You have enough problems of your own but thank you for offering. Anyway, I must be going those cows won't milk themselves. Though sometimes I pray that they would."

Isabelle watched as Polly made her way over to the cows which her children were slowly herding into the milking barn. She was filled with gratitude for her own lot in life. She had a roof over her head, and a future with Nico. She would never have to worry about pennies ever again.

It was cruel that the families of the men who had died in battle were now being left to fend for themselves. England was no home for heroes. If anyone deserved justice it was the likes of Polly and her children.

Nothing was fair. Society had dictated somewhere in the dim and distant past that women were not entitled to a fair or equitable existence.

As she began to walk back toward her home, Isabelle made a decision. Polly and her children may not have found justice, but she would. Phillip Prescott was going to pay for his crimes.

Chapter Twenty-Two

"Are you sure about this? If things go awry Donovan will not hesitate to act."

Nico took a seat next to Isabelle in the carriage. It was a risk taking her with him to confront Phillip Prescott, but he found her unwilling to budge once she had made up her mind.

"You gave me the choice of what was to be done, and this is what I have decided," she replied.

Donovan looked out the window. His right hand was tucked inside his coat pocket, no doubt holding the handle of his pistol. Nico hadn't made mention of the gun to Isabelle, nor the pistol and knife which were inside his own coat.

Prescott may come quietly and give no fuss, but Nico had been in enough skirmishes in the rough back streets of Rome to know that a cornered man was a dangerous beast. He was taking no chances with Isabelle's safety.

As Nico knocked on the front door of Prescott's elegant home in Broad Street, Donovan stood to one side of the door out of sight.

Nico leaned in to Isabelle. "Just taking precautions. Donovan knows what he is doing."

When the butler opened the front door, Nico didn't wait to be offered admittance, he stepped across the threshold and stood over the butler. "I am Count Nico de Luca. Where is your master?"

"In the downstairs drawing room, with Mrs. Prescott. I shall announce your arrival your lordship," he replied.

The butler scurried ahead, with Nico and Isabelle close on his heels. He had barely got the words out as to who had been at the front door when Nico brushed past him and swept into the room.

Prescott who was seated next to his wife on a couch got immediately to his feet.

"Your lordship we were not expecting you, may I offer you some refreshments?" he said.

With a flourish Nico pulled out the title deed for New Cavendish Place and threw it on the table.

"Let us dispense with the pleasantries, shall we? I have been through the books of account for the past five years and have a very clear picture of what you have done. Add to that the recent visit I paid to a certain gambling establishment in Brighton and I think you can guess why we are here."

Prescott's face turned ashen, while on the couch his wife let out a cry of dismay. They all turned to see Donovan enter the room. No one failed to see the cocked pistol he held in his hand.

Prescott nodded toward the butler. "We won't be requiring any tea. Close the door after you."

As soon as the butler had gone, Donovan locked the door. Nico stifled his anger over Donovan's display of the gun. He was a firm believer in letting words get him what he needed. Violence and threats of it were to be used sparingly. Donovan by his actions had at least got everyone's attention.

"Would you please take a seat so we can discuss this like civil people," replied Prescott, his gaze still fixed firmly on Donovan's pistol.

Isabelle and Nico each took a seat on the matching couch opposite the Prescott's.

"You may wish for your wife to leave the room," offered Nico.

As soon as he had entered the room, Nico's gaze had fallen on the large swell of Mrs. Prescott's stomach. From his time spent in the company of his married sisters, he guessed that she was close to full term.

Prescott took a hold of his wife's hand and patted it gently. "Rosemary knows everything. She will stay."

His wife nodded her agreement.

Nico clenched his jaw. This was not how he had intended for the encounter to happen. With both Isabelle and Mrs. Prescott present he would have to measure his words carefully. The last thing anyone needed was for Donovan to go waving his pistol around while in the presence of two women, one who was heavily pregnant.

Nico shot Donovan a look which had him backing away and taking a place next to the now locked door. No one would be coming or going until Nico gave the order.

Prescott sat forward on the couch, his hands held loosely together.

"I don't know if this will hold any weight, but I never intended to steal from anyone. I have been an honest man all my life. I worked hard to achieve my position with your company," he said.

Nico let the comment rest. He had dealt with enough liars in his life to know that when caught they usually began with a self-serving speech. Prescott it would appear was going to stay true to the liar's book.

"I began to play cards as a small entertainment, as many other people do. Somewhere along the way I lost myself in them. The losses began to accumulate and I found myself in the unenviable position of owing money to some rather unsavory people. After I paid those debts I should have stopped. I should have learned my lesson but I didn't."

Rosemary Prescott began to cry. Soft sobs which made her pregnant stomach rise and fall. Nico chanced a look at Isabelle on the couch beside him. Her face was a study of stony expressionlessness. She was giving nothing away.

Donovan shifted on his feet and cleared his throat. Prescott stiffened his posture at the obvious message.

"I took the money from the company accounts over several years. I thought that by the time anyone from the de Luca family came to visit England I would have won it all back at the card table and no one would be any the wiser," said Prescott.

"But you didn't count on the repercussions that forcing Anthony's hand that night in Brighton might bring. Did you?" said Isabelle.

Prescott looked at her briefly, but quickly averted his gaze.

Coward. You ruined her life, but you cannot look her in the eye.

"There is nothing I can say that will make any of this better. Anthony and I played each other quite regularly. He was a good chap. Perhaps a little too emotional about his gambling, but then again who am I to judge? The main thing is that the money I stole from you was repaid and I haven't touched the cards since," replied Prescott.

A spark of pure rage lit in Nico's brain. The self-important arrogance of Phillip Prescott was breathtaking. As far as Prescott was concerned as long as the money had been repaid, the rest was someone else's problem.

Nico would have seized Prescott by the throat if Isabelle had not reached out and placed a hand on his knee.

"So, you admit to stealing from the de Luca family?" she said.

A look of surprise appeared on Prescott's face at her words. The theft of money from her house hold guest should not be of any concern to her.

Nico placed his hand over Isabelle's, grateful for her intervention. She was speaking on behalf of him, knowing he was struggling to control his temper.

She was also sending Nico a strong, private message. Her

concerns were that of a family member. He looked at her. *Mia moglie forte. My strong wife.*

"Yes. I did steal from the count. But I paid it back in full. With the value of the house that I won fairly from Anthony Collins I have more than repaid the debt. I am a changed man. I have other more important things in my life now," replied Prescott, looking at his still weeping wife.

Isabelle released Nico's hand and got to her feet.

"I think we have heard enough," she said.

Nico and Donovan exchanged surprised looks. Donovan shrugged and put his pistol back in his coat pocket.

For the first time since the beginning of their visit Nico was suddenly wrong footed. Isabelle was calling the meeting to an end, but without having settled anything. His moment of praising her as a strong wife vanished in a puff of confusion.

What the devil was she thinking?

The Prescott's too seemed taken aback by Isabelle's words. Rosemary Prescott, wiped her tears away.

"What is to happen to my husband?" she asked.

Nico got to his feet and took hold of Isabelle's arm. He snatched up the title deed for the house and hauled Isabelle toward the door. He was not going to risk allowing her to have the last word without his say so.

"This matter is not over with yet. I suggest you have your papers and affairs put in order forthwith Prescott. It goes without saying that your employment is terminated," said Nico.

Donovan unlocked the drawing room door and followed Nico and Isabelle out of the house. Outside in the street Nico helped Isabelle into their waiting carriage before taking Donovan aside.

"I don't know what Mrs. Collins is playing at, but Prescott must not be allowed to try and make a run for it. I want you to put together a team of reliable men and have the house watched day and night. If Prescott looks like he is going to attempt to flee

London, you send for the Bow Street Runners. I will have him arrested first then decide what is to be done. That *bastardo ladro* will not make a fool of me a second time."

Donovan nodded his understanding, bastard translated across both languages.

Chapter Twenty-Three

"What just happened?"

Nico closed the carriage door behind him and threw himself onto the seat opposite Isabelle. She saw the look of angry confusion on his face. It was to be expected. He had thought he was controlling matters, and she had suddenly taken command.

"I told you we needed to talk to him. To get to the truth. That is what we have done," she replied.

Nico threw his hands up in obvious frustration. "Yes. And we just walked out of there without anything being resolved. If I was Prescott I would be laughing long and loud right now. He probably thinks he got away with it. I thought you wanted justice," said Nico.

She held his gaze. The Isabelle of the past who would have sat and meekly said nothing was gone. She had been offered a say in what was to become of Phillip Prescott and she was damned if she was going to let Nico run roughshod over that just to suit his purposes.

"I do want justice. And before we walked in that room I was more than prepared to have him arrested. But that was before," she replied.

Before she had set eyes upon the heavily pregnant Rosemary Prescott. The moment she saw Rosemary, Isabelle knew there had to be another way for her to find justice.

"You saw her. You saw his wife. If Prescott stands trial for fraud, he will hang. Where will that leave Rosemary Prescott and her unborn child?"

Nico shook his head.

"And what about you? Do you think either of them give a damn about you or what you and Ann have been through? All this time they have known the dire straits you have been in and yet they haven't once tried to help you," he replied.

She was no fool. Nico was more than likely correct in his estimation of the Prescott's but Isabelle couldn't bring herself to wield the final blow. Not yet.

"You may think me a weak female but that is not true. I just want to be sure that justice if it is to be served it done with mercy. English justice can be very black and white. Our courts are only too eager to either hang people or transport them to the colonies. Can there be another way is all that I am asking," she said.

Nico huffed. One thing Isabelle had learned about him from their short time together was that he didn't like arguments. Nico was happy when everyone wanted to do things his way, but he became noticeably uncomfortable when challenged. She was under no illusion that their tempers and characters would make for an interesting marriage.

"I understand your position, so will you allow me to refer the matter to a lawyer? I can try to find another way for Prescott to face justice. A way that does not carry the death penalty," Nico replied.

Isabelle thought for a moment. The idea was fair. They both got a little of what they wanted without having to cede any real ground.

"Agreed. We will refer the matter to a lawyer and not make any final decision until we have discussed it. You must also realize that if a trial does come of this, you may have to delay your journey home to Italy," she replied.

"Yes. I had already come to that conclusion. The only way for matters to be expedited would be for Prescott to plead guilty. From the way he talked I doubt very much that he has that in mind."

Nico took off his hat and ran his fingers through his hair.

"Can we agree on something else?"

"Yes?"

He moved across the carriage and sat down next to her. Reaching over he placed a tender kiss on her lips.

"Can we agree that we won't allow every conversation we have to be all about this one thing. It is almost Christmas. I would like for you and me to be able to spend some time talking about us and coming to an agreement about our plans to marry. Because we are getting married," he said.

Isabelle lifted her face to his and returned the kiss. Her lips held the offer of more than just a discussion of marriage.

"I shall think about it. Of course, you would have a much more compelling argument to get my agreement if you would show me what you are offering," she purred.

He pulled her hard against him.

"When we get home, I shall show you every inch of what I am prepared to give you," he growled.

Chapter Twenty-Four

Nico waited until Isabelle had gone back to her room before climbing out of bed. Tonight, he held back his normal protestations at her leaving his bed.

At the corner of New Cavendish and Harley Streets Donovan was waiting for him. "Nice evening for a spot of night work," observed Donovan.

Nico scowled. He would much rather be still tucked up in bed with a warm and naked Isabelle beside him. But there was work to be done. They climbed aboard a plain black hack and gave the driver instructions.

A while later they alighted a hundred yards from the de Luca shipping offices. As they passed by a small laneway, a group of three men stepped out from the shadows. They silently followed Nico and Donovan.

At the gateway to the offices the small party stopped. Donovan turned to the men. "Now, he is not a big man but with his liberty at stake you can expect he will fight like a mad man. I want two of you to wait out here just in case he gives us the slip. If he does, you are to grab him and place him under formal arrest," he said.

He handed an official looking document to the nearest man. "The warrant was signed by a magistrate earlier this evening. Please check it to make sure it is in order. My master is from an Italian noble family and we would not want any diplomatic problems with the envoy from the Vatican," he said.

Nico kept his gaze on the upper window of the shipping office. A small light could be seen moving about upstairs.

"Come on let's get this done. The sooner we have Prescott in custody, the sooner the lot of us can go home to bed," he said.

While two of the Bow Street Runners waited in hiding in the street below, Nico and the others headed inside. The night watchman met them at the gate. When he saw Nico with two strangers in tow, he frowned.

"Good evening my lord, my apologies I wasn't expecting you. Mr. Prescott didn't mention that you would be here this evening. He arrived a short while ago, said he had some papers to collect. Shall I go on ahead and announce your arrival?" he said.

Donovan took the man by the arm and guided him toward the gate.

"My good fellow, we are going to be here for a little while so how about you head home early this evening. As you can see Count de Luca is here, so no one is going to be breaking in and stealing anything tonight," said Donovan.

Nico nodded his approval and the night watchman bowed low.

"Why thank you my lord. That is very generous of you. Much appreciated," he said.

As soon as the night watchman was gone, Nico started for the stairs. At the top of the stairs the Bow Street Runner halted and silently drew his pistol from the folds of his coat.

Phillip Prescott didn't turn at the creak of the door.

"Stop creeping around the offices man and get back to your post," he snapped.

Nico and Donovan exchanged a knowing look. "You can stop looking for the papers you thought you had hidden in the wall behind the cupboard. They were removed this afternoon," said Nico.

Prescott slowly turned. At the sight of two pistols being pointed at his head he lifted his hands in surrender.

"I was just getting some final papers," he said.

Donovan shook his head. Nico sighed.

"I have been dealing with the likes of thieves, swindlers and even pirates for a great deal of my life. You people never change. As soon as I uncovered the first fraud I had Mr. Donovan's people go through the rest of the accounts. A man of your station can hardly afford to live in Broad Street, unless he has other means of supplementing his income. You have been skimming off the top of all the shipping invoices for years from the look of it. Your pathetic performance this afternoon may have fooled Mrs. Collins and perhaps your wife, but all it did was further convince me that you are an unrepentant thief who belongs in prison," said Nico.

Prescott's gaze drifted to the door. The silent question which hung in the room being one of whether he was going to risk making a dash for the stairs.

Donovan chuckled. "I dare you. I bloody well dare you."

Prescott's shoulders sank. The battle was over before a shot had been fired. When the Bow Street Runner stepped into the room and clasped iron shackles on his wrists Prescott said nothing.

"Phillip Prescott you are charged with unlawful breaking and entering of a place of business. You will be taken to Newgate prison and face a magistrate at the earliest convenience," he said.

Upon hearing what he was being charged with Prescott looked at Nico in surprise. It was only as they got outside and he was about to be led away, that he pulled back on his restraints and spoke.

"Would you do me a kindness and send word to my wife. She will know how to contact my lawyer," he said.

Donovan snorted in obvious disgust, but Nico nodded his agreement. If they were going to see justice done, Prescott deserved to be defended.

Chapter Twenty-Five

✻

The following morning Nico rose at his usual late hour of eleven. He was tired of the cold. Only a mad man would willingly be out before the day had a chance to get any warmth into it.

Dressed and freshly shaven he went in search of Isabelle. He dreaded the encounter. Informing her that he had waited less than a day to break their agreement and have Prescott arrested would not go down well with her. But it had to be done.

"Cosi sia," he muttered opening the sitting room door.

Ann and Isabelle often spent their mid mornings enjoying the winter sun which streamed in through the large upstairs window. The room however was empty. He headed downstairs. He located the butler coming up from the lower kitchens, wiping a stray piece of food from his mouth. Nico stifled a huff. The man was forever eating. He was certain the butler ate more than his wages in food.

"Have you seen Mrs. Isabelle Collins this morning" he asked.

The butler nodded. "Yes, both Mrs. Collins have gone out this morning. I believe they have gone shopping for Christmas gifts," he replied.

Christmas. Damn.

Christmas in England meant the exchange of gifts on Christmas Day. In Italy presents were not handed out until Epiphany well after the new year. Christmas Day was only three days away. He had nothing to give to either Ann or Isabelle.

"Did the ladies take my carriage?" he asked.

"Yes."

He turned and raced for the stairs. "Go and hail me a hack outside. I shall retrieve my hat and coat. I have Christmas shopping to do."

❧

The crush of crowds in the street of London kept Nico out until late that afternoon. By the time he returned to New Cavendish Street he was in a foul temper.

He was certain that there were people in London who thought it fine sport to take an hour to decide exactly what color handkerchief would do for a Christmas gift for their maiden aunt. All the while they made certain not to notice the frustrated Italian gentleman standing behind them who wished to pay for his selected purchases and have them wrapped without delay.

With his carefully chosen gifts hidden out of sight at the back of his wardrobe he went to speak to Isabelle. The sooner they had the difficult conversation about Prescott the better.

Isabelle as could be expected, did not take the news well. Nico stood rooted to the spot as Isabelle unleashed her fiery temper on him.

"You swine! All your promises in the carriage home yesterday were barefaced lies. I expect you had absolutely no intention of keeping to your word," she roared.

"That is not true. I hadn't intended to...," he stammered.

"Save your lies Nico. I have heard them all before and from a far more accomplished liar than you," she said, cutting him off. Isabelle stormed out of the sitting room, slamming the door loudly behind her.

A red-faced Nico was left alone with Ann. She rose from her chair by the fireside and came to his side.

"If there is one thing I would caution you never to do. Never lie to Isabelle. I am ashamed to say that Anthony was a master of the false tongue. She has heard every plausible and implausible story that you could think of to tell," she said.

He turned to Ann. "So, what am I to do? She has to understand what happened and why I had Prescott arrested."

It would be bad enough if he had intended to break his word all along but upon discovering that Prescott intended to flee London he had been left with no other option but to have him arrested. Isabelle had to understand.

"My suggestion would be to leave her alone for the rest of the day and let her temper simmer down. She can be a fiery little thing at times, but her moments of anger don't normally last long. Talk to her after supper, she should be in a more receptive mood by then."

"I have a dinner engagement this evening, if Isabelle is still awake when I return I shall try to speak to her then," he replied.

Nico was tired and after a day spent out in the crush of the Christmas crowds and now out of sorts with Isabelle, the last thing he wanted to do was to venture out on the town again. But a friend of his father was visiting London and he was obliged to spend an evening with him.

Chapter Twenty-Six

Fortunately, the evening he did spend with the family friend was exactly what Nico needed. Hours being able to converse in his native Italian brought a calmness to his mind. That and several bottles of good Italian wine. Apart from an over exuberant fellow diner who managed to spill a whole glass of wine down the front of Nico's shirt and jacket, he had had a wonderful evening out.

Climbing the stairs to the upper floor, he first checked in on his room. Isabelle was not waiting for him in his bed. He growled with frustration. He wanted nothing more than to curl up in bed with her naked in his arms.

"You will listen," he muttered.

He knocked on her bedroom door and waited. Then he knocked again.

"I have nothing to say," she said opening the door. When her gaze fell on his wine stained shirt tears sprang to her eyes.

"You men are all the same. You lie. You get drunk. And fools like me are expected to smile and go on as if nothing was wrong. If this is how you truly are Nico, then go back to Rome and leave me be. I won't do this again," she said.

She pushed the door, but Nico's strategically placed boot stopped it from closely.

"No," he said.

The wine haze cleared from his mind. He was not leaving until Isabelle acknowledged that he was not like Anthony. He never would be.

He stepped into the room and closed the door behind him. He locked it and dropped the key into his trouser pocket. Isabelle glared at him.

"You are going to listen to me without interruption. Sit down," he ordered.

She marched over to a chair near the fireplace and slumped down in it. She harrumphed her obvious displeasure at being told what to do in her own bedroom.

"Good. Now here is the truth of the matter. Prescott never stopped stealing from me. He simply changed his method. When we visited his house yesterday I was not surprised that he only mentioned the theft of the money which he covered by winning this house. The other money which he has been skimming from every shipment that passes through the de Luca offices was less easy to discover," he said.

She sat up in the chair and looked at him.

"Go on," she said.

"Donovan engaged a special accountant to review the books over the past few days. Prescott was unaware that some of the books had been removed from the offices. Fortunately, I have other staff in the office whose discretion can be relied upon. All told we estimate he stole nearly three times the value of this house."

"Which would explain the grand house he owns in Broad Street. I must confess to being a little surprised that a man of his station could afford such a place. He must be quite wealthy," she replied.

Nico took a seat in the chair opposite Isabelle, sensing she was slowly coming around to his side.

"I didn't intend to have him arrested so soon. You and I agreed on a way forward and I had already engaged a lawyer to work though the legalities of what could be done. Unfortunately, Prescott was not going to wait to see what our next move was, he booked passage on a ship to the United States of America yesterday not long after we left his house. If I had not had him arrested, he and his wife would be on the high seas at this very minute."

"And your money with them," replied Isabelle.

She looked away and stared long into the fire. Nico reached out and took hold of her hand. He knew her well enough to know that she wanted to apologize for having accused him of lying to her, but he would have to be the one who opened the door for her to step through. It would take time for her to trust in men again, but he was determined that she would always trust him.

"I know what it looked like, and I know you have been hurt too many times before. But believe me, the last thing I ever want to do is to lose your faith in me. I love you Isabelle. I want us to have a marriage based on truth and trust. You are going to have to accept that I am not Anthony."

She looked at him with sad eyes. He hated seeing her this way.

"I'm sorry. I shouldn't have viewed you through the same lens that I did with him. You did the right thing in having Prescott arrested. I was wrong to accuse you of lying to me. I lived through so many nights of Anthony coming home in a disheveled state that my response just now was out of ingrained habit. But from the sound of you, you are not drunk," she replied.

He looked down at his wine stained garments. "I had dinner with a family friend. One of the other guests got a little carried away with an amusing tale and the next thing I knew I was wearing the contents of his wine glass. No harm done. You will find us Italians to be an expressive group of people," he said.

His heart filled with hope when Isabelle nodded.

"Yes, it is one of the reasons why I love you Nico. You are not afraid to show how much you love life," she replied.

He started to get to his feet, but Isabelle rose quickly from her chair and pushed him back down. On her face he saw the reappearance of the sultry smile she reserved for their sexual encounters. He went hard when he heard her next words.

"You will find that at times we English can also be expressive. Lay back and let me demonstrate," she said.

Isabelle dropped to her knees before Nico. His mind immediately filled with the darkest desire for her. He bent down and placed a hot kiss on Isabelle's inviting lips.

When they broke from the kiss, she pushed him back in the chair, bringing her hand to rest on his stomach.

"Close your eyes and let me attend to you," she purred.

One wicked thought now took front of stage in Nico's mind as Isabelle tugged on the placket of his trousers.

Please.

Her nimble fingers soon had the buttons free and he felt the cool night air kiss the skin of his groin. His heart pounded in his chest. He swallowed deep in anticipation as he lay back in the chair and closed his eyes.

"Oh," he groaned as she took his manhood into the hot heaven of her mouth. Her hands came to rest on either side of his hips. He reached out with a trembling hand and placed it gently on top of her head.

She needed no guidance in her work. She sucked and pulled in a natural ebb and flow of love making. He opened his eyes and looked up at the ceiling, praying to the heavens that this woman would remain forever in his life.

With every stroke the tension rose higher. He looked down at her, watching with sensual fascination as her head rose and fell. Isabelle was truly gifted in the art of loving a man.

Sensing the inevitable was close, he gently took hold of her hair and pulled her away from him. When she looked up, Isabelle's eyes were glazed with passion.

Nico took a deep breath and tried to cool his blood. He needed to take control of his body in order to extend the life of this encounter. To give Isabelle everything she desired.

"Come to me," he whispered.

He helped her to her feet. She lifted the edges of her nightgown, then with her legs straddled either side of his hips she sank down taking the full length of him inside her.

He took hold of the front of her night gown and after roughly untying the laces, he ripped the bodice open, baring her breasts to his sight. Her nipples hardened in the chill of the air. He took hold of one breast and brought it to his mouth. As her nipple slipped past his lips, Nico suckled hard. Isabelle whimpered. He suckled hard once more.

"Nico, oh god," she moaned.

He pushed her legs as wide apart as the chair would allow, before withdrawing from her and then thrusting deep into her once more. The chair held Isabelle in place. She was perfectly seated for him to torture her breasts as he settled into a rhythm of thrust and withdrawal.

"Touch your other breast. Show me you know how to pleasure yourself," he instructed.

When she rolled her nipple between her fingertips Nico rewarded her with a hard thrust that had her sobbing with need. He did it again and the expression of pleasure on her face told him he had found the golden path to her climax.

He built the tempo of their union slowly, controlling every stroke. Fully intending that when she was finally ready to come, Isabelle would be begging for him to complete her.

Her hands slipped from her breast and came to rest on his shoulders, he lay back and she began to ride him. His heart soared. This was the passion and the connection he had always yearned for with the woman in his life.

There were no veils between them. This was an honest moment between two people in love. A mutual sharing of bodies and aching need.

Isabelle's breathing shallowed and Nico sensed she was close to the end. He pushed her back and roughly took hold of her breast.

"Come for me, take all I can give you Bella," he said.

He took her nipple between his teeth and gently nipped. She gripped his shoulders hard and rode his deep thrusts with sobbing desperation. He ground his manhood against her mons matching her thrust for thrust.

Isabelle came in a rush of whimpers and pleasured sobs. He wrapped his arms around her holding her tight. Then slowly he brought his strokes back to a gentle rhythm.

She kissed him, and he felt the wet of her tears on his cheek. The final barriers between them were gone. Their gazes met as she sat back and looked at him.

"Thank you," she whispered.

He chuckled. After what she had done to him with her lips it was he who should be showing gratitude.

"Now, let me show you how much you mean to me Isabelle. Let me make love to you."

He lifted her from the chair and placed her kneeling on the floor in front of him. He lifted the remains of her nightgown over her head and tossed it aside.

"Lay your head down. Open yourself fully to me," he said.

He moved behind her and pushed her legs open. Slipping two fingers into her wet heat he began to stroke deeply. When his fingers touched the edge of her sensitive nib she whimpered. She was ready for him.

"I am going to show you what you mean to me Isabelle. What we can be together," he said.

Placing his hands on her hips he slowly entered her. When he was fully seated within her, he paused for a moment before slowly withdrawing. He entered her again. With his arm wrapped around her waist he held her close as he thrust slowly in and out. "You are mine Bella. Surrender your heart to me, I will always keep it safe," he vowed.

Isabelle's sobs of submission echoed in the room. She was his, complete in her surrender to his tender loving. They could battle it out in the sitting rooms of the world, but in the bedroom, he would reign as her gentle master.

His climax came in a blinding rush. Long after he had come, he continued to thrust slowly in and out of Isabelle unwilling to break the bond.

When their bodies finally returned to the world, Isabelle led Nico to her bed. He stripped the rest of his clothes from his body and pulled her to him. With her head resting on his chest they drifted off to sleep.

As he closed his eyes he heard her whisper. "I love you Nico. You are my life."

"Ti amo Bella," he replied.

Chapter Twenty-Seven

"Come on, get up. I have something to show you."

Nico opened a lazy eye. He reached for Isabelle, but she was too quick and darted out of reach of his searching hand.

"We don't have time for that this morning. I need you to come with me," she said.

During the long night while Nico had slept deeply beside her Isabelle had lain awake and pondered the situation. While they were close to agreement on their combined future, there was still the matter of what to do about Phillip Prescott.

He deserved to serve at least some prison time, but she was adamant that he would not hang. His unborn child had done nothing to deserve growing up without his father.

She found it frustrating that while she had fallen for Prescott's pitiful act, Nico had seen right through it. But no more. Prescott was going to pay for his crimes and she knew exactly how to hurt him.

"Could we please have some breakfast first? I am not the best person in the morning until I have had my coffee," pleaded Nico.

"No. Go to your room and get dressed, I shall see you downstairs in ten minutes," she said.

He sat on the edge of the bed and gave her a sultry pleading look which had her reluctantly shaking her head. He was not going to lure her back into bed. Tempting though it was, especially after the events of the previous night.

"Later. If you are a good boy," she said.

"And twice if I am a very good boy," he replied.

He climbed off the bed and retrieved his trousers. Isabelle gave a quick check of the hallway to ensure there were no servants about before Nico made a dash for his room.

She chortled as he raced bare foot along the hallway and disappeared. He had just closed his bedroom door when Ann appeared at the top of the staircase.

"How are you this morning?" she asked.

Isabelle was in two minds as to what to say. By rights she should be telling Ann of the latest revelations about Anthony and Prescott, but the hopeful smile on Ann's face stopped her.

Nothing she could say would change the fact that Anthony was dead. No good would come from telling Ann that Anthony had lost the house in a game of cards and then killed himself. Isabelle decided to leave matters as they were. Ann deserved to have some kind memories of her only son.

"I am well. Nico and I had a long discussion last night and have resolved a number of issues. Suffice to say we are back on good terms. I am taking him for a walk to see the market gardens, we shall join you for breakfast when we return," she replied.

Isabelle caught up with Nico downstairs a short time later. "I have something to show you, after which I would like your opinion," she said.

When they reached her favorite tree in Green Lane, Isabelle took Nico by the hand and led him over to the edge of the field. She pointed to the women and children who were working the market gardens.

"People forget that while the allies won the battle at Waterloo, it came at a great cost to the widows and orphans of our fallen soldiers. I know a number of these families and they are all living hand to mouth at best," she said.

Living so close to the edge, she knew it would only take one small disaster for any number of these families to find themselves begging on the streets of London. Nico looked out to where she was pointing and nodded.

"Yes, and with the crop failures that have been occurring across Europe I expect they will find things even more dire in the months to come. Even the crops around Rome have struggled this year. While I understand your concerns, I do not understand what this has to do with you getting justice from Prescott?" he replied.

She turned to him. "I would expect that considering the situation Prescott currently finds himself in, that he would be more than willing to consider an offer of financial settlement in return for you dropping the charges against him. I need money to help these people and Prescott is going to give it to me."

Nico chuckled, "Now that is more like it Bella. Hit him where it hurts most. In his bank account."

The brief smile disappeared from his face. "Now you might not like what I am going to say, but I shall say it anyway. I want you to let me handle this."

Words of protest were on her lips as Nico pointed a finger at her.

"You caved when we went to his house. He played you. If you want to help these people, then you have to let me do it. Trust me to help get you the justice you and these people deserve."

She looked down at his finger, forcing herself to resist the temptation to bat it away. Stubborn male that he was, she also knew he was right. She needed him to push Prescott into making a deal.

"Alright. But I want not a penny less than a thousand pounds," she replied.

"Agreed."

Chapter Twenty-Eight

Newgate prison was as foul as Nico had imagined. It was over crowded and stank of all manner of human waste. As he climbed down from the carriage the next morning inside the main prison courtyard, he pulled a handkerchief out of his coat pocket and covered his face.

He turned to Isabelle whose face reflected his own response to the hell hole that was the overcrowded prison.

"Don't bother. I know it stinks but I am not staying in the carriage. I am coming with you. The sooner we get this deal sorted, the sooner we can both leave," she said.

The third member of their party had to be dragged from the carriage. Prescott's private banker was more than a little reluctant to step inside the prison proper.

"I must protest your lordship. Couldn't I just wait outside the gates and you bring me the signed papers?" he said.

Nico took him by the arm. "No. I need you to confirm that your client has executed the proper instructions to settle this matter. If Mrs. Collins can stand to step inside so can you," he replied.

Inside the main prison building they were shown to the dank, dark cell where Phillip Prescott was being held. The look of surprise on his face at seeing Nico and Isabelle turned to outright shock when he saw the man who had accompanied them.

"What the devil is going on?" he asked.

"I have a proposal. It will require the settlement of funds, hence why I brought your banker with me," replied Nico.

Prescott's banker stood with his satchel of papers clutched tightly to his chest. His gaze continually darting around the prison cell. The Duchy of Lazio had powerful connections within the London based diplomatic community; and so, the man from the Bank of England had been given his instructions to attend Newgate prison without delay.

Nico nodded at the banker, who fumbled around in his satchel before passing a document through the prison bars to Prescott. He quickly read it, then thrust it back at his banker.

"Absolutely not," he said.

Isabelle looked at Nico, but as agreed she remained silent.

"I thought that might be your initial response. Well then, let me put it to you in terms of gambling parlance. I am upping the stakes a little. You either sign that document or I go to the magistrate and have the new charges of fraud and embezzlement added to the current ones you are facing," he said.

The man from the Bank of England looked at Nico with fear in his eyes, then turned back to his client. "Mr. Prescott as your banker I strongly suggest you consider the offer from Count de Luca. You can always find a way to make back the money. But if you are found guilty of fraud you will hang," he said.

Prescott glared at Nico. Contempt was evident on his face. "Half the amount and not a penny more," he sneered.

Nico stood for a moment and considered the offer, then he nodded to the banker.

"I accept your client's offer. Amend the paper and have him sign it. Once I have written confirmation that the money has been transferred to Mrs. Collins I shall instruct my lawyer to press ahead with only the minor charges. I am sure your well-paid lawyer will be able to plead for a short sentence," he said.

Isabelle stepped forward and smiled sweetly at Nico as he took her arm.

"Thank you, my love," she said.

She turned to Prescott. "One man is already dead because of your greed so it serves no purpose to see you hang. Your money however will do a lot of good for others. That is the justice that I want," she said.

Nico's heart swelled with pride as he led Isabelle out of the prison cell and away from Newgate. Once they were away from Newgate Prison and its foul air Isabelle rewarded Nico with a kiss.

"Well that was better than nothing. Five hundred pounds should help to see those families through the next few years. Though I was surprised that you agreed to settle on half the amount for which I asked. Prescott did not have a lot of room with which to bargain," she said.

Nico chuckled.

"My love. I didn't ask for a thousand pounds. I knew that even with his life on the line Prescott's pride wouldn't allow him to settle on my first offer. What he finally agreed to was exactly what I wanted. Later today five thousand pounds will be deposited into an account bearing your name."

He received a second kiss for his efforts.

Chapter Twenty-Nine

With the matter of Prescott now settled, Isabelle turned her attention to the final hurdle of settling her future with Nico. The matter of where they would live.

She looked across at him and smiled.

"Nico. About England," she said.

He sighed.

"I hated every day I was here as a child. No sun, no warmth. I missed the food of my homeland. La Dolce Vita. Unless you are from Rome, you cannot possibly know how much it is in your blood. But if living in England is what it takes to have you in my life I will do it," he replied.

The pain in his voice was heartbreaking. Nico's love for her was so great that he would sacrifice his own happiness for Isabelle.

Isabelle shook her head. Never again would he have to give up a part of his soul for the sake of someone he loved.

"In my darkest hours I gave up hope of ever sharing love again. Nico, you have brought the light of love back into my life. I shall come to Rome with you. I want to build a new life with you, to bear your children. If that means leaving here then so be it," she replied.

She reached over and brushed a tear from his eye. Nico took hold of her hand and raised it to his lips.

"I shall need to visit England more often to keep an eye on business matters and you will come with me. Though never again in winter. I draw the line at another English winter, it freezes my Roman blood," he replied.

Isabelle nodded. If Elizabeth de Luca could find a way to live between two countries and keep the love of her husband, then her daughter in law could do the same. Their lips met in a soft kiss of confirmation. When Nico finally released Isabelle from his embrace, he held both her hands.

"Isabelle Collins ti amo. Would you do me the greatest honor and be my wife? My Contessa de Luca. I shall keep you safe and you will never want for anything ever again. If you allow me to love you and gift me your love in return, I will do everything within my power to make your life a happy one," he said.

As marriage proposals went it was more heartfelt than anything she could ever have imagined.

"Yes Nico, I will marry you. You already have my heart."

Chapter Thirty

❧❦❧

Nico placed Isabelle's arm in his as they left the house. The walk to the Austrian embassy was a short one. Ann walked a step behind.

"It is a three-minute stroll at best, I think I can manage that without a gentleman holding my arm," she said.

Isabelle looked back over shoulder to her soon to be former mother in law. Ann was still sporting the grin that had sat on her face since Isabelle and Nico shared their wonderful news.

As light snow began to fall, Nico stopped and looked up. "It doesn't snow in Rome very often, I hope you will not miss it too much," he said.

Isabelle shook her head. She was looking forward to long summer days and warm nights in Rome. Nights she would be able to share with her husband.

As they turned the corner into Queen Ann Street they were greeted with the sight of dozens of carriages lining either side of the street. A crowd was gathered outside the front door of Chandos House. When they drew closer Isabelle could hear the rumble of people talking in many different languages.

"I didn't realize that there would be so many people here," she said.

Nico nodded. "The Austrian ambassador has special permission to allow certain rooms in Chandos House to be consecrated as a Roman Catholic church on holy days. Since England doesn't have many Catholic churches we Catholics have to make do with temporary ones. And being Christmas Eve there are a lot of us needing somewhere to take Mass," he said.

Isabelle chanced a look at Nico as they walked under the small portico above the entrance. His gaze was fixed firmly ahead, but she caught the glint of pride and happiness in his eye. He was about to present his chosen bride to the world.

"My father's connections in Rome ensured that we secured an invitation to the Christmas Eve service," he said.

They followed the other assembled guests into an elegant but spacious drawing room. Rows of chairs were lined up for the service. At the end of the room a temporary altar had been erected. A red cloth, embroidered with a gold crucifix hung over it.

Nico guided Isabelle and Ann to their seats.

"I must go and speak with Monsignore Abato and the Austrian ambassador before the service, I shall return shortly," he said.

Ann reached out and took a hold of Isabelle's hand as Nico walked away.

"Well who would have thought this is where you and I would be on Christmas Eve this year," she said.

"I cannot believe that in a short while Nico and I will be married," replied Isabelle as tears welled up inside.

A new life with Nico beckoned, but she would never forget the depths of loneliness and despair she had lived through over the past few years.

Ann squeezed Isabelle's hand. "I am so happy for the both of you. And while I am losing you as my daughter in law, in my heart you will always be my daughter. I am proud of you for having chosen to risk your heart again. Nico is a good man," she said.

"Are you certain you won't come to Rome with us?" replied Isabelle.

Ann smiled. "Nico has already offered for me to have the best cabin on any of his ships travelling to Italy. I simply have to ask his new business manager. But as I have a widows and orphans trust to help administer now, plus a house full of servants to manage you cannot expect me to be dashing off to the continent whenever it takes my fancy. I shall come to visit you in good time. Of course, you will always be welcome at New Cavendish Street if you wish to bring my grandchildren to England to visit me," she replied.

Nico returned and took his seat next to Isabelle. She shook her head when he looked at Ann and raised an enquiring eyebrow. "I tried, but Ann is staying in England," she said.

"The ambassador, Prince Esterhazy has confirmed that since this is the Austrian Embassy and the laws of the Holy See apply here, Monsignore Abato can marry us. When we get to Rome his holiness Pope Pius will give us a blessing," he said.

At the end of the Christmas mass a short time later, Prince Esterhazy rose and addressed the assembled guests.

"My friends and fellow worshippers. I would ask for you to stay a little while longer. Tonight, we celebrate Christmas as a time of new life and new beginnings. Marriage is also about creation of a new life, that of husband and wife. Please join me in wishing Count de Luca and Isabelle Collins the very best of futures together. Monsignore Abato will now conduct the wedding service."

A thrill of excitement mixed with a helping of nerves gripped Isabelle as Nico took her by the arm and they walked to the front of the room. Her new royal blue gown was matched perfectly by the sapphire earrings which she wore. The same earrings she had refused to take from him on the journey to Higham Place.

As they stopped in front of the priest, Nico leaned in. "Ready for the grand adventure?" Isabelle nodded. He was her future now. Her vision of watching their children playing on a sunlit beach was no longer an impossible dream.

Hand in hand they stood and faced each other as they said their vows. Isabelle looked deep into Nico's eyes as the priest gave them the final blessing. Nico smiled back at her.

"Ego conjugo vos in matrimonium, in nomine Patris, et Filii, et Spiritus Sancti. Amen. You may now kiss the bride," said Monsignore Abato.

"Finally," said Nico as applause rippled through the room.

He stood for a moment. Isabelle waited patiently. This would be their first kiss as husband and wife, and she knew he would want it to be perfect.

"I love you Bella," he said.

"Ti amo Nico, ti amo."

Chapter Thirty-One

ROME, JANUARY 1816

The Duke of Lazio's Palace.

Nico let go of Isabelle's hand. "Wait for a moment my love, I want to surprise him," he said.

She smiled as he walked ahead of her and into the sunlit open space that was his father's study. She stood back against the wall, hidden by the shadow of the afternoon sun. Lorenzo de Luca had his back turned to them, he was busy shuffling papers.

"Papa, I am home," said Nico.

Lorenzo whipped around and Isabelle saw the light of joy on his face at the sight of his eldest son.

"Nico! Oh, my boy. il mio bellissimo ragazzo!" he cried.

He pulled Nico into a heartfelt embrace, while Isabelle stood and wiped tears away. Her husband had been as nervous as a young boy on the coach journey from the Port of Civitavecchia to Rome. She understood why. It was not every day that a man brought home his new bride to meet his family. A bride that they had no idea existed.

"How was England? I hope it was not too difficult for you. And how was Richard and Eugenie, did they like the painting of your mother? Are they coming to visit us again soon?" asked Lorenzo.

Nico nodded, then turned to Isabelle who stepped forward out of the shadows.

"I brought someone back from England with me," he said.

Isabelle walked confidently toward her new father in law and dipped into an elegant curtsey.

"Bonjourno, tua grazia, il mio nome è Isabelle de Luca," she said.

Nico smiled at her faultless Italian. During the past week on the ship bound for Italy, she had practiced the first words she would say to Lorenzo over and over. The Italian phrase book Nico had given to her for Christmas had served its purpose well.

Lorenzo stood and looked at her for a moment. Then his face crumpled. Tears ran down his cheeks, and he pulled Isabelle into his embrace.

"La mia bellissima figlia," he said.

Nico came to his side and gave his father a gentle pat on the back. When Lorenzo pulled away he was laughing.

"I told my foolish son to go to London and find love. It turns out he was not so foolish after all. He found you. Oh, and you are so beautiful Isabella. Welcome. Welcome to our family. I can see from the look on your face that you love Nico with your whole heart and that is very good," he said.

She turned to her husband and smiled.

"Yes. I do love Nico with my whole heart, and he knows it too."

Chapter Thirty-Two

Thank You

T hank you so much for reading this story and I hope you loved it as much as I did when I wrote it.

If you did enjoy this book, then please consider leaving a short review on the book retailer site from where you purchased this book.

Stay in Touch

If you would like to hear about my latest releases, special offers and competitions please sign up for my newsletter. www.sasha-cottman.com

Come and say hi at these places:

Facebook www.facebook.com/SashaCottmanAuthor

Goodreads www.goodreads.com/author/show/7136108.Sasha_Cottman

Bookbub www.bookbub.com/authors/sasha-cottman

My Books

For the full list of my books please visit www.sashacottman.com/

Love Sasha xxx

Turn the page to read the first chapter of book one of the Duke of Strathmore series, *Letter From a Rake*.

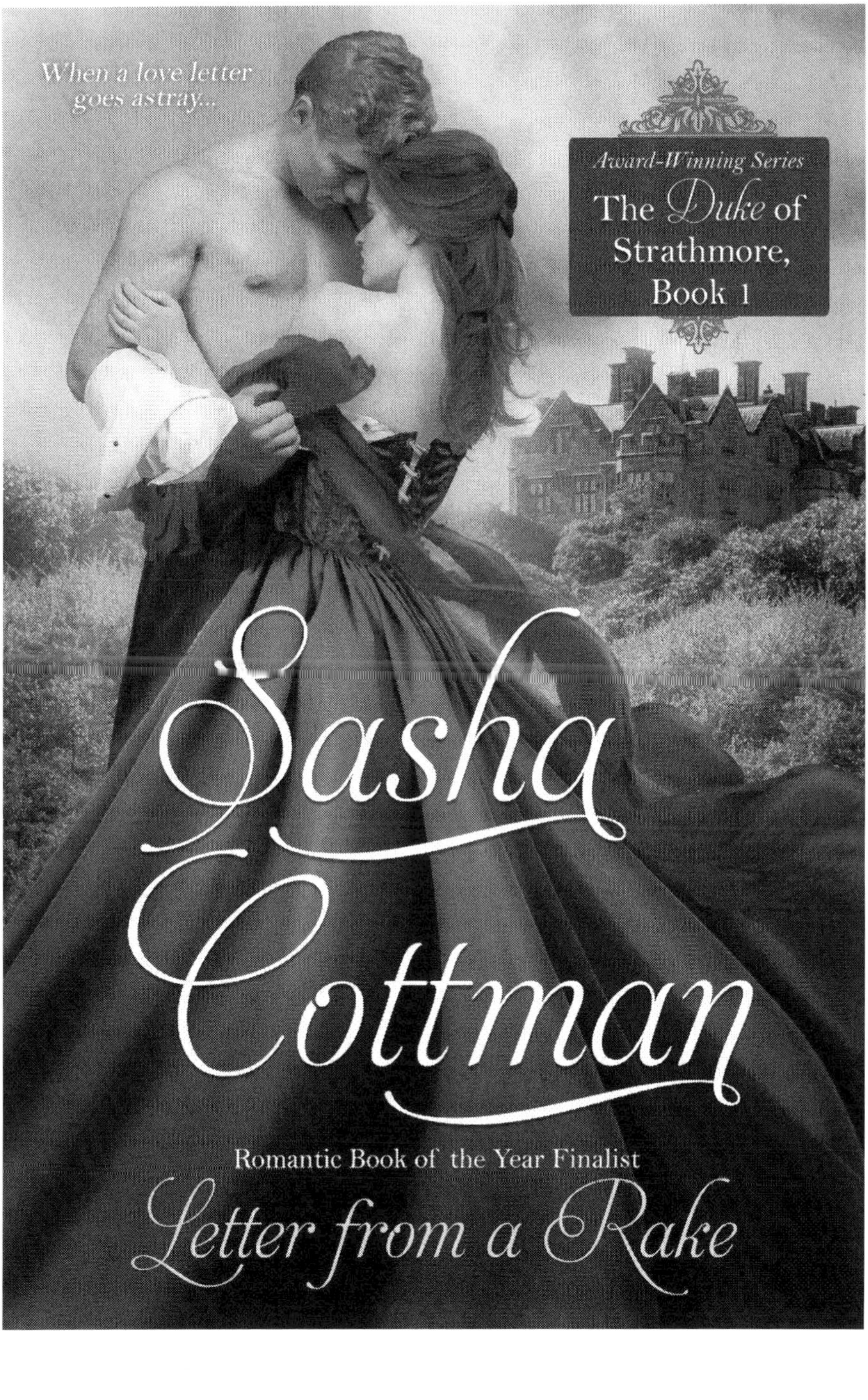
When a love letter goes astray...
Award-Winning Series
The Duke of Strathmore, Book 1
Sasha Cottman
Romantic Book of the Year Finalist
Letter from a Rake

Chapter One: Letter From a Rake

London, 1817

At three o'clock in the afternoon, on the eighth day after her arrival in England, Miss Millicent Ashton made up her mind. She wanted to go home.

The snide remarks had begun the moment she and her mother entered Lady Elmore's spacious drawing room.

'So that's what an Indian elephant looks like,' whispered a blonde miss by the window. She leaned in close to another girl, who giggled.

'I wonder if she gives free rides.'

Millie knew the cruel taunts were aimed directly at her.

In the other homes, they had so far visited, she had managed to perfect the art of removing her coat and sitting down in one motion. With luck, she was usually able to seat herself in the corner of a couch and hide partially behind the skirts of her mother.

Unfortunately, this time Lady Elmore had greeted them at the drawing room door and Millie had suffered the humiliation of being presented by her mother in the middle of the room, where of course everyone could take in Millie's ample frame.

While the two older women remarked on how cold the weather was in England compared with India, the first of the whispers began.

The giggling misses' barely concealed mirth earned them both a steely stare from Millie's mother, who ushered her daughter to a couch to be seated next to their hostess.

Millie's heart sank. Now everyone in the room could see her. As Violet took the seat beside her, Millie gave her mother a half-smile, silently regretting her mother's need to make a statement.

For the rest of the two-hour visit, she sat quietly between the two women, taking the occasional sip of her black tea and politely refusing to partake of the delicious array of cakes Lady Elmore's servants had laid out on the low table before them.

With her hands folded in her lap, she focused on the pain of her thumbnail boring deep into her palm. She would poke her own eyes out before she would show any kind of response to the cruel taunts.

She retreated into the comfort of her own private thoughts, slowly and methodically naming the fjords of the Norwegian coastline, and when she was done, she started on Finland. Nothing soothed her mind more quickly than attempting to tackle mental tongue twisters.

When her mother finally began making her farewells, Millie was lost somewhere in the far frozen north of Scandinavia.

A whispered 'Millie, we are leaving,' roused her.

With a well-practiced curtsy, she politely thanked Lady Elmore and followed her mother to the front door. Hands clasped tightly in front, she kept her gaze firmly fixed on her gloves.

After attending several of these events since their arrival in London, she had learnt the painful lesson of what would happen if she risked one last glance around the room of vipers. At Mrs Wallace's house earlier in the week she had caught several of the girls puffing their cheeks out at her as she left. One had even managed to poke out her tongue before smothering the action with a well-timed cough.

&.

As soon as the carriage door closed behind them, she turned on her mother.

'That is the last of those horrid things you drag me to; next time you can go on your own,' she snapped, stamping her foot for good measure.

Violet Ashton let out a sigh. 'And what am I to tell the ladies of London society when my highly eligible daughter does not accompany me on these outings?' she replied.

'Tell them you have locked me in my room for swearing, or better still tell them that I went mad and you had me put me away in Bedlam.'

She crossed her arms, glared out of the window and continued.

'If they want to see me they can pay the keeper a coin. I barely know these people and yet they choose to judge me purely by sight. Not one of those simpering misses has attempted to speak to me. No, they would rather just make fun of a newcomer; well, it's the last straw.'

'Don't say it,' her mother replied.

'Say what?'

"I want to go home to India, I hate this place, all the people are horrid and it's cold." If I hear those words from your lips one more time today, I swear I shall get on a boat myself and go back to India just to get away from you.'

Violet pulled her coat tightly around herself and let out a tired sigh.

'Honestly, Millie, my ears cannot take many more of your complaints. Don't think I don't know how unkind those girls are, but you have to remember you pose a threat to them and they don't like it. They are trying to bring you down to their level. You just have to rise above them.'

Millie sat staring at her mother, too stunned to speak. For the first time since their arrival, she was lost for words. How could she possibly be a threat to anyone?

Finally, she shook her head. 'How am I a threat to those girls, Mama?'

Violet gave a knowing smile and nodded her head.

'You are from a good family; your father and uncle are powerful men and you come with a sizeable dowry. A lot of those girls have only their passing beauty to catch a potential husband and most men want more than that,' she explained.

Millie scowled. 'Yes, but most men want a slender, elegant wife who stays out of their way,' she replied, knowing she would never be that sort of woman.

Her mother laughed. 'Where on earth did you get such a silly notion from? Have you ever seen me shy away from your father? And believe me, I have never been thin in my life.' She leaned forward on the leather bench and brushed her hand gently over Millie's cheek.

'Darling, you will find that different men are attracted to different things. Some will find you a little unusual because of your foreign upbringing and not to their taste, but I assure you there will be someone who finds you the most enchanting creature he has ever laid eyes upon. And when he discovers the witty, intelligent girl that you are, he will give thanks you have come into his life.'

She tucked a wayward lock of Millie's chestnut-brown hair behind her daughter's ear before adding, 'Of course, you will have to stop complaining about England for him to have a chance to appreciate your finer qualities, but I am sure you will soon over-come your aversion to the place; everyone does eventually.'

'Apart from the French,' Millie muttered, knowing she was testing her mother's patience to the limit.

Violet sat back in her seat and rubbed her temple. She had

complained of a throbbing behind her left eye before they'd arrived at Lady Elmore's and Millie knew from the pale color of her mother's cheeks that one of her serious headaches was imminent. As soon as they reached home she would retire to her room and have a long afternoon sleep, leaving Millie once more alone to amuse herself.

Her mother's words of advice still hung in the air. Violet was right, of course; Millie would have to make peace with her new home but, as for the other matter, her mind was wracked with doubt.

No one in London would think her wonderful or stunning. It would take a special man to look beyond the obvious and see the real Millie Ashton. From what she had seen of London society so far, she doubted that such a man existed anywhere in England.

As the carriage made the short journey to their new home in Mill Street, Millie continued to look out the window. The cobbled streets of London were a stark contrast to the dusty streets of Calcutta, the city where she had been born.

Instead of the hot windy streets full of people, animals and hand carts all attempting to make progress through the oncoming traffic, London was the picture of ordered civility. The few people walking on the streets of St James made their way on stone pavements, not in the middle of the road. And there were no cows wandering lazily in and out of the street stalls and markets.

Millie sat back in her seat and, closing her eyes, tried to recall the cries of the *khonchavala*, as they walked the streets of her home city peddling their many wares.

Once they'd reached home and were inside, Millie quickly handed her bonnet and coat to her maid. The house call had been long and trying, her temper was frayed and she knew if she stayed near her mother for a minute longer, harsh words would be exchanged and the whole day would be a complete shambles.

She brushed a kiss on her mother's cheek, wished her a speedy recovery and with purpose headed downstairs in search of the kitchens.

Millie was sitting in the big wooden cook's chair with a mug of hot sweet tea, slowly chewing on one of Mrs Knowles' mawa cakes when she saw her brother Charles' head appear around the kitchen door.

Stepping into the kitchen, he was greeted by the Indian born Mrs Knowles with a respectful *'Namaste'*. He bowed in return, before turning to his sister.

'Thought I might find you in here. How was the visit to Lady Elmore's?' Charles asked, as he stopped near the kitchen table.

His gaze drifted to the plate sitting next to Millie at the end of the table. A single cake sat alone among the scattered crumbs.

'Oh dear, that bad?' he replied, running a hand through his sandy blond hair.

Millie wiped her mouth with a cloth napkin and slurped down the last of her tea. Small tears formed in her eyes and she bravely blinked them away. Rising from the chair, she managed to maintain her composure for the seconds it took for her to fall into her older brother's embrace.

He wrapped his comforting arms around her and held her close.

'They called me an elephant,' she said as the tears found their way to her cheeks. 'None of them wanted to talk to me; they just sat and giggled behind their hands. They were simply horrid.'

Charles stroked her hair and planted a kiss on the top of her long brown locks.

'Millie, you just have to give them time, let them get to know you, and I promise things will get better. Not everyone here is horrible. You will have lots of friends in no time. We've only been here a week, you cannot dismiss all of London just yet,' he said with a sigh.

Millie sniffled back the tears and took the handkerchief he offered.

'I know, I know; Mama says exactly the same thing, but—'

'But what?'

'London isn't what I was promised. Where is the sophistication, the elegance? So far all I have seen are drawing rooms full of small-minded harpies,' Millie replied, pulling out of his embrace.

Charles shook his head.

'I hope you are not setting your mind against our new home?'

She shrugged her shoulders. 'It's just that I had hoped London might be a bit more cosmopolitan. I know many of the English in Calcutta tended to be indifferent to the rest of the country, but I suppose I expected a little more from all that I had heard of England. It is harder to find my feet here than I had expected.'

'But, you have to admit, it's not all been bad. You cannot tell me you have not enjoyed shopping for new clothes, Millie. I have twice tripped over piles of boxes in the front hallway,' Charles replied.

'No, the shops are simply wonderful. I have never seen anything like them. I am sure one could shop for days and not venture into the same store twice,' she replied, grateful for the change in topic.

'Good and what about the museums? I know you have a long list of galleries, gardens and castles you wish to visit.'

Her spirits rallied at the idea as she looked at her brother and nodded. They were both going to have to find their way through the maze of London society in the oncoming months.

'Thank you, Charles. You are possessed of the happy knack of finding the good in every situation. I can always rely upon you to pull me out of a miserable mood. And you are right; I shall ask Papa if he will take me to see Lord Elgin's Greek marbles when he next has some spare time. I hear they have moved them to a new display room.'

'Good. You could ask him on the way to the party tonight,' he replied.

A wave of nausea came over her. Whether it was as a result of the large number of spiced cakes she had eaten, or from the realization that tonight her family were to be guests of honour at a 'Welcome home' ball, Millie couldn't tell.

Millie thanked Mrs Knowles for the cakes and headed for the door. As he passed the table, Charles snatched up the last remaining mawa cake, stuffed it into his mouth and followed his sister from the room.

Also by Sasha Cottman

The Duke of Strathmore Series

Book 1: Letter from a Rake

Book 2: An Unsuitable Match

Book3: The Duke's Daughter

Book 4: (holiday novella) A Scottish Duke For Christmas

Book 5: My Gentleman Spy

Book 6: Lord of Mischief

London Lords Series

An Italian Count for Christmas

www.sashacottman.com/books

Printed in Great Britain
by Amazon

28926948R00097